CW00505318

CHARMING A COWBOY KING

Copyright © March 2023 by Katie Lane

All rights reserved. Except for use in any review, the reproduction or utilization of this work in whole or in part in any form by any electronic, mechanical or other means, now known or hereinafter invented, including xerography, photocopying and recording, or in any information storage or retrieval system, is forbidden without the written permission of the publisher.

This book is a work of fiction. Names, characters, places, and incidents are a product of the writer's imagination. All rights reserved. Scanning, uploading, and electronic sharing of this book without the permission of the author is unlawful piracy and theft. To obtain permission to excerpt portions of the text, please contact the author at *katie@ katielanebooks.com*

Thank you for respecting this author's hard work and livelihood.

Printed in the USA.

Cover Design and Interior Format

© THE KILLION GROUP INC.

Charming a COWBOY KING

KINGMAN RANCH
· 7 ·

KATIE LANE

To Sue Boren, and all the amazing stepmamas and stepdaddies out there who have opened their hearts and changed the life of a child forever

CHAPTER ONE

"LOVE POTION PIE? Now that's a pie I'll have to try." The truck driver in the grease-stained ball cap winked flirtatiously. "Of course, I'm already half in love, sweetheart."

It took every speck of willpower Paisley Grayson Stanford had not to snort in disgust. She wasn't disgusted with the flirting trucker as much as the entire concept of love. At one time, she'd believed in fairytales and happy endings, but not anymore. Love was for naïve fools and Paisley was through being a fool.

Completely ignoring the trucker's comment, she pasted on a smile and repeated the order. "That's two Coors beers and two slices of Love Potion Pie. I'll have that right out."

She turned and headed toward the bar that covered one entire wall of Nasty Jack's. Multicolored Christmas lights hung above it year round, but tonight, there was also a long banner of pink paper hearts and red cupids. Below the banner, cuddling couples whispered sweet nothings to each other completely unaware of the pitfalls looming on their love horizon.

At the end of the bar, a group of cowboys had congregated around the redheaded bartender, hoping to gain her attention. They had it, but they would learn that Everly's attention wasn't always a good thing.

Stepping up to the bar, Paisley watched as her sister efficiently filled beer glasses . . . while putting the cowboys in their place. Unlike Paisley, Everly had no problem stating her mind.

"Don't complain to me about not having sweethearts on Valentine's Day when there are plenty of women in this bar who would love to spend the night two-stepping with a handsome cowboy. Now stop standing here wasting your time with a happily married woman and get to asking or I'm going to start serving you gutless wienies Shirley Temples instead of beer."

All three cowboys looked thoroughly chastised. As soon as they got their beers, they slunk away.

Everly walked over to Paisley and rolled her eyes. "Men. They complain about not being able to get a woman when they're not willing to make the effort it takes to get one. Even your son has more guts." A smile spread over her face. "I guess Henry told you about Brooklyn Ann 'the prettiest girl eber.'"

Paisley laughed at her sister's impersonation of her son. Henry had just turned five and still struggled to pronounce his *v*'s. But that certainly didn't stop him from talking.

Although lately he hadn't been talking to Paisley.

"Who's Brooklyn Ann?" she asked.

"I guess she's a pretty little blonde he met in his preschool class. He sweet-talked me into buying him the biggest Valentine card at Cursed Market to give to her."

Henry hadn't said a word about the card or the little girl. While Paisley greatly appreciated everything Everly had done for her and Henry—taking them in when they first arrived in Cursed, finding them a place to live, giving Paisley a job, and watching Henry while Paisley was dealing with the train wreck of her life—she couldn't help feeling a little jealous of how close her sister and son had become.

Of course, she couldn't blame Henry. Everly was vivacious and fun and strong. She would have never put up with a man abusing her. She would have left Jonathan the first time he'd hit her. Unlike Paisley, who had allowed the abuse to go on for years. It had taken Jonathan threatening Henry to finally get her to leave. Otherwise, she would probably still be with him.

Which was just weak and pathetic.

"Okay, what's that frown all about, Paise?" Everly cut into her thoughts. "It's not a big deal Henry didn't tell you about his girlfriend. What kid wants to talk to their mother about girls?"

Paisley set her tray on the bar. "Lately, he doesn't seem to want to talk to me about anything."

"Now I find that hard to believe." Everly took jars of maraschino cherries and green olives out of the mini fridge and started refilling the garnish tray. "Your son is the biggest chatterbox this side of the Pecos."

"With everyone but me. He doesn't even like being around me anymore."

"That's not true. He adores you." Everly sent her a stern look. "Probably because you spoil him rotten. Just because he throws a tantrum doesn't mean you should give him what he wants, Paise."

"I don't always give him what he wants." When Everly lifted an eyebrow, she conceded, "Okay, so I have spoiled him lately. But only because he's been through so much."

"He's okay, Paise." Everly reached out and squeezed her arm. "So are you."

Paisley wished that was true. She didn't feel okay. She felt like an untethered helium balloon that was floating away. But, as always, she put on a good front.

"You're right. We're both fine. Just fine." She glanced around and changed the subject. "So where is Chance? I thought for sure he'd be here tonight hanging out with his favorite valentine."

A dopey look came over Everly's face at just the mention of her new husband. "He's at home making a late dinner for us . . . and I hope preparing for a naughty night of sex." Her hazel eyes twinkled. "When I married a preacher, I never thought he would be so adventurous in bed. Did I tell you about what we did the other night? Chance got two of his silk ties and tied me to a chair and then he—"

Before she could finish, Kitty Carson yelled from where she sat at the end of the bar. Kitty delivered the mail and gossip to the townsfolk of Cursed, Texas. She had a helmet of stiff red hair and a voice that could be heard in three counties.

"Everly! Can I get another margarita? Potts says he only drinks beer, but when I came back from the ladies' room my drink was suspiciously gone and his kisses taste like tequila and lime." She waved at Paisley. "Hey, Paisley! I have an official-looking package for you. I'll bring it to you first thing tomorrow."

Paisley felt all the blood drain from her face. She knew what was inside the package. Divorce papers. While a part of her was relieved her nightmare marriage was almost over, there was another part of her that mourned the loss of all her hopes and dreams for a happily-ever-after.

"Another margarita is coming right up, Kitty," Everly said. "I'll make one for Potts too." After she grabbed two margarita glasses from the shelf behind the bar, her gaze caught Paisley's. "You okay?"

She nodded. "I'm fine." But how could a person be fine when they had figured out that happily-ever-afters were only in fairytales? "Now I better get two bottles of Coors and two slices of Love Potion Pie back to those truckers."

Everly set the glasses down and pulled two beers out of the cooler. Once they were opened, she placed them on the tray. But instead of hurrying back to the kitchen like she normally did and returning with the pie, she sent Paisley a sad look. "I'm not taking your food orders back to the kitchen anymore, Paise. I get that you have an aversion to men after what happened to you. But I think it's time you got over it. I hired you as a waitress and that includes working with the cook—even if you don't particularly like him. So stop being a wienie like those cowboys and face your fears."

As much as Paisley wanted to argue, she couldn't. Not only because she hated confrontation, but also because Everly was right. She shouldn't expect her sister to run the bar and take orders back to the kitchen. It was Paisley's job and she needed to start doing it.

Leaving her tray on the bar, she headed to the swinging door that led to the kitchen. She hesitated for only a second before she pushed her way through. The kitchen smelled like a mixture of sautéing onions, frying French fries, and spicy wings. The person responsible for those smells stood at the cooktop with his back to Paisley.

Hayden West.

Just the sight of him had Paisley's stomach tightening.

To say Hayden rattled her was an understatement. Everly was right. She did have an aversion to men after Jonathan's abuse. But her reaction to Hayden wasn't just wariness. He also made her feel . . . exposed. Like his deep cobalt-blue eyes could see right through her fake smile and calm façade to the scared, insecure woman beneath. While he joked and teased with Everly, he spoke to Paisley with formal respect like she was his Sunday school teacher.

Although she doubted he had spent much time in Sunday school.

From what Everly had told her, Hayden was

an ex-bronc rider from Montana who'd started drifting around the country after his rodeo career cratered. He'd wandered into Cursed by accident and decided to stay awhile. During the day, he worked as a ranch hand for the Kingman Ranch, and four nights a week, he ran the kitchen at Nasty Jack's. And ran it well. Paisley had tasted his cooking and he knew his way around a stove.

Which was obvious by watching him now. He was well over six feet tall with broad shoulders and biceps that stretched the sleeves of the Nasty Jack's T-shirt he wore, and yet, he moved with graceful efficiency as he pulled wings from the fryer and placed hamburger patties on the flat top.

His hair was a deep chestnut brown, cut short in the back and on the sides with the top longer. When he wasn't wearing his black Stetson, like now, a couple stray locks fell over his forehead. He was ruggedly handsome with his deep-set blue eyes, high cheekbones, and square jaw that was always covered in dark stubble. Not that Paisley cared about handsome men. Jonathan had taught her beauty was only skin deep.

But plenty of other women noticed Hayden. Whenever he stepped out of the kitchen, every woman in the bar stopped what she was doing to watch his copper-stitched Wrangler pockets pass.

"Ms. Stanford?"

She lifted her gaze from Hayden's butt to find him looking over his shoulder at her. Steam rose around him from the burgers sizzling on the cooktop, causing the locks on his forehead to curl like two backward C's. He had obviously caught her checking his butt out, but his eyes didn't hold a twinkle of cockiness. They held the same look they always did when he looked at her.

Sympathy.

It was that sympathy, coupled with the way he rattled her, that caused her dislike of the man. The last thing she wanted was sympathy. Especially from a saddle tramp.

She stiffened her spine, hiked her chin, and spoke in a haughty voice. "I need two slices of Love Potion Pie." He studied her with his clear midnight eyes as if he knew she was struggling to hold his gaze and keep up her fake bravado. Just when she was about to call chicken and look away, he did.

"Yes, ma'am. Two Love Potion Pies coming right up." After wiping his hands on the dish towel tucked into his jeans, he moved to the prep island where a cluster of pies sat. Wolfe Kingman owned Nasty Jack's and his wife, Gretchen, made all the pies from scratch. Besides beer and margaritas, they were the bestsellers at the bar. People came from all over Texas to get a slice of Gretchen's pies.

With an efficiency that was surprising for a man with such large hands, Hayden sliced into the tower of toasted meringue covering the top of the pie and plated a slice. Beneath the thick meringue was a layer of dark chocolate custard on top of an even darker chocolate crust.

"I think I might like this pie better than the chocolate peppermint pie Gretchen made for

Christmas," he said without looking up. "Have you tasted it?"

"I don't like chocolate."

He hesitated for a brief second before he sliced another piece of pie. "I don't think I've ever met a woman who didn't like chocolate. So what is your favorite pie?"

"I don't have a favorite. I don't like sweets."

His gaze finally lifted. His eyes held surprise. "No peanut butter cookies, coconut cake, apple pie, strawberry shortcake?" When she shook her head, he continued to toss out desserts. "Tiramisu, hot fudge sundae, mud pie?"

"No."

He looked at her as if she was a puzzle he couldn't quite figure out. Or a weird anomaly that made no sense. "Not even candy as a kid?"

"We weren't allowed to eat candy."

Again, she read sympathy before he looked away. "Everly mentioned that your parents were strict."

Strict was putting it mildly. Paisley and Everly's parents had been rigid perfectionists with high expectations. Paisley had tried to meet those expectations. Everly hadn't. It was obvious which daughter had made the right choice.

"I don't really have time for conversation," she said. "I just need the pie."

He nodded before he picked up the plates and moved toward her. Try as she might, she couldn't stop herself from taking a step back.

He froze. His gaze locked with hers for a long,

uncomfortable moment before he turned and set the plates back on the prep island. "I'll just let you get those. I need to check on my hamburger sliders before they get too well done."

Relieved, Paisley quickly grabbed the plates and headed for the door. But before she could get there, Hayden stopped her.

"Paisley."

It was the first time he had used her given name. He always called her Ms. Stanford. For some reason, hearing *Paisley* spoken in his husky voice made her feel even more unnerved.

She gripped the cold plates and tried to keep her voice steady and calm. "Yes?"

After a slight hesitation, he spoke. "I get why you're leery of men, but I just want you to know that I would never hurt you."

CHAPTER TWO

ONCE THE DOOR swung shut behind Paisley, Hayden released a long sigh.

She was scared of him.

He knew she didn't like him. That had been easy to figure out from the way she went out of her way to avoid him. But he hadn't thought she was afraid of him. Damn, if the fear he'd seen in her eyes hadn't just broken his heart . . . and pissed him off. Once again, Hayden wished he'd gotten a few punches in the night he'd had Paisley's husband in his grasp. Of course, that would only make Paisley fear him more.

She was like an abused horse. She only knew what she'd been taught. She'd been taught that men hit when they got angry. In order to change her mind, he had to prove to her that he wasn't like Jonathan.

He shook his head.

Whoa there, cowboy. You don't need to prove anything to Paisley. She's not your problem.

Except she *was* his problem.

Hayden had never believed in love at first sight. He'd never believed that a person you hadn't even spoken to could suck your breath right out of your lungs and make you feel like you were having a heart attack. Mostly because, after thirty-two years of life, not one woman had ever made him breathless or his heart beat out of control.

But then one day, a breathtaking woman with piles of sunshine hair and eyes the color of a Montana spring meadow had walked into his life and changed his entire concept of love at first sight.

When he first set eyes on Paisley Grayson Stanford, he'd thought he was going to fall right off the horse he'd been riding. Of course, he almost did fall off when Paisley charged the horse and it reared, causing him to struggle to keep his seat in the saddle while holding Henry. He'd found Henry wandering the ranch and was bringing him back to his mother and Aunt Everly. Paisley was not happy about her son running off. Or about him being on "a beast" of an animal with a strange cowboy. A cowboy who yelled at her for frightening his horse.

If Hayden could go back and change their first meeting, he would. But he'd learned there was no going back in life. You could only go forward. Except there was no going forward with a woman who hated men. He knew that because he had eavesdropped on the Grayson sisters' conversations more than once. It was hard not to when the kitchen door was as flimsy as paper and Everly and Paisley usually sat at the bar when they had their sister talks.

Paisley had made it very clear she didn't want anything to do with men.

Ever.

Which left Hayden pretty well screwed.

And it was probably for the best. He had never intended to stay in Texas. Montana was his home. His mama and stepdaddy, Jimmy, were there. And so was the chunk of land he'd bought for his horse ranch. Coming to Cursed had only been a whim. Or maybe not a whim as much as something he needed to do before he could move on with his life.

The smell of burning hamburgers pulled him from his thoughts and he hurried over to the cooktop to find all the sliders burned on one side. That's what he got for daydreaming about a woman who was too damaged by her past to give him a second glance.

He threw the ruined burgers in the trash and made some fresh ones. He had just finished placing them on the cooktop when the back door squeaked open and a little boy in Spider-Man pajamas, a cowboy hat, and boots strutted in.

"Hey, Hay!" He tipped up his hat and flashed an adorable grin at Hayden.

Henry James Stanford didn't stand much over three feet tall. He had blond hair like his mama and golden eyes like Everly. Like his aunt, the kid could talk a rattlesnake out of its skin and never pulled punches.

He wrinkled his freckled nose. "Whatcha cookin', Hay? It smells like dog poop."

Hayden wiped his hands on the dish towel

tucked in his belt. "I think the better question is what are you doing here?" He glanced at the clock. "At nine twenty-three on a school night? Shouldn't you be in bed?"

"I was in bed. Hessy tucked me in real tight and read me my fa-borite story, *Little Blue Truck*. I'm gonna habe a truck one day. All cowboys habe trucks. You habe a truck and Buck has a truck and Delaney has a truck and Stetson has a truck and Wolfe has a truck—"

Before he could go through the entire King-man family, Hayden cut him off. "Does Hester know you're here?"

Hester Malone lived in the two-story farmhouse across the street from Nasty Jack's. According to the neon sign in the front window, she read palms and told fortunes for a living. At first, Hayden had been a little leery of the silver-haired woman who always wore black and had unusual purple eyes. But once he'd gotten to know Hester, he discovered she was just a nice lady who had con-vinced the townsfolk she was psychic. She rented rooms to Paisley and watched Henry when Pais-ley had to work.

"Well," Hayden said when Henry still hadn't answered. "Does Hester know you're here?" The guilty flush on the little boy's cheeks was answer enough. Hayden removed the dish towel from his belt. "Okay, partner, let's get you back before Hester realizes you're missing and calls the sher-iff."

"But I need to talk to you, Hay. It's important." Henry's hazel eyes filled with tears. If anything was Hayden's kryptonite, it was kids' tears. And women's. And horses'. Okay, he was a sucker for tears in general.

He sighed and lifted Henry to a stool at the prep counter. "Okay, shoot. But make it quick. We need to get you back to Hester's."

Henry squished up his face. "I got woman troubles."

Hayden rubbed the scruff on his jaw to hide his smile. "That's certainly something that will keep a man up at night. I'm assuming this has to do with Brooklyn."

"Brooklyn Ann. She likes to be called by two names just like me."

"So what's going on with Brooklyn Ann?"

"Well, I got her a nice balentine just like you told me." His face fell. "But Brendan got her a great big candy bar. And I guess Brooklyn Ann likes chocolate more than cards 'cause she squealed real loud when she pulled that candy bar out of her balentine bag and she only smiled when she saw my card." He looked confused. "I thought girls didn't like chocolate. Mama doesn't."

Hayden sat down on the stool next to Henry. "Well, your mama is the exception to the rule. But just because Brooklyn Ann loves chocolate that doesn't mean she likes Brendan more than you."

"It doesn't?"

"Nope. So you can't bow out just yet. You need to stand your ground and don't let Brendan get the best of you just because he gave her candy. And here's the thing. Once she eats that candy bar, it will be gone. But the card you gave her, she can keep forever."

"Foreber?"

"Yes, sir. Girls love keepsakes. My mama keeps all the cards and letters people have given her over the years." Including the ones from Hayden's father. She had tied the notes and cards into a neat stack with a ribbon and given them to Hayden when he turned eighteen. As a sullen teenager, he'd thrown them all away. He regretted that now. Even if his biological father hadn't wanted to know him, Hayden still had a longing to know his father.

Which was how he had ended up in Cursed.

Henry's face lit up. "Thanks, Hay. You are the smartest cowboy eber."

Hayden reached out and tapped the brim of Henry's hat. "I don't know about that. You're a pretty smart cowboy."

Henry's face fell. "I'm not a cowboy. Cowboys ride horses and my mean mama won't let me ride a horse."

As if on cue, Mean Mama walked in through the door. Paisley's green eyes filled with confusion when she saw Henry sitting there. If tears were Hayden's kryptonite, Henry was Paisley's. She adored her son . . . some might say a little too much. Henry had her tied right around his little finger. All the kid had to do was show any sign of being unhappy and Paisley gave him whatever he wanted.

Although she didn't look like she was in the giving mood at the moment.

"What's going on?" she asked.

Henry voiced Hayden's thoughts to a tee. "Uh-oh."

"Uh-oh is right, young man." Paisley strode into the kitchen, letting the door swing closed behind her. "What are you doing here? Where is Hester? And don't you dare tell me that you snuck out and came here by yourself."

Henry's eyes got big and Hayden stood and tried to smooth things over. "I was just going to walk him back home."

Paisley turned on Hayden and her eyes flashed green fire. "Without telling me he'd snuck out of Hester's house and crossed a busy street in the middle of the night? He could've been killed."

Before Hayden could defend himself, Henry slipped off the stool. "No, I couldn't, Mama. I looked both ways just like you taught me. Left, then right, and then left again, and then right again."

"That's good," Hayden said. "But your mama's right. You still shouldn't have crossed the street by yourself. Or snuck out of Hester's without telling her." He looked at Paisley. "And I would've told you about him being here."

She gave him a look that said she didn't believe him for a second before she turned back to Henry. "You're in big trouble, mister."

Henry didn't look worried. "But I needed to talk to Hay, Mama."

"About what?"

"About man things and you aren't a man.

You're my mean mama who won't let Hay teach me how to ride a horse."

Paisley's gaze snapped over to Hayden and he held up his hands. "I never mentioned teaching him how to ride."

"But you would teach me, wouldn't you, Hay?" Henry looked at his mother and his bottom lip puffed out. "If my mean mama would let you."

"Now, partner—" Hayden started, but Paisley cut him off with a look that pretty much said, *"Stay out of it. This isn't your business,"* before she took Henry's hand and marched him right out the door.

Once the door slammed behind them, Hayden sighed. That hadn't gone well. Not well at all. And she was right. She and Henry weren't any of his business.

Now all he had to do was convince his heart of that.

After he finished plating the sliders and delivered them, he checked in with the other tables to see if anyone needed anything. He figured Paisley wouldn't be back for a while. When he stepped behind the bar to fill some drink orders, Everly glanced at him with surprise.

"Shouldn't you be closing up the kitchen and leaving?" Nasty Jack's stopped serving food at ten o'clock and Hayden usually left after he finished cleaning up.

"We had a little incident." He grabbed some whiskey glasses. "Henry decided to sneak out of Hester's and pay me a visit. Paisley took him back and I thought I'd cover for her until she gets him settled."

Everly shook her head as she filled shot glasses with tequila. "Damn, that kid reminds me of me. I guess Paisley was ticked."

"Not at Henry as much as me. I'm not sure if she hates me because she thinks I'm responsible for her son's preoccupation with cowboys or just because I'm a man."

Everly capped the tequila bottle and turned to him. "She doesn't hate you."

"She sure doesn't like me."

"She doesn't like any man right now. But she'll get over that once the divorce is final. Which could be soon. Kitty said an official-looking envelope came in the mail today for Paisley. Hopefully, it's the divorce documents all signed, witnessed, and sealed. But . . ." The concerned look in her eyes had Hayden finishing her sentence.

"But you can't see the abusive asshole making it that easy for her."

Everly shook her head. "You saw him the night he came to Cursed looking for her. He treated her like a possession, not a wife. Men like Jonathan don't let go of their possessions easily."

Hayden remembered the night well. He had planned on taking Everly to dinner in Amarillo just as a friend. Hayden had figured out early on that Everly had a thing for the town preacher. But when Hayden had gotten to the church to pick Everly up, she hadn't been there, and Hester Malone had told him she had gone to Hester's house because Paisley was in trouble.

The trouble was Paisley's husband. Jonathan Stanford had come to town to get his wife . . . and punish her for leaving in the first place. Just the thought of the man's fingerprints on Paisley's throat still made Hayden feel a little crazed. He needed to take a few deep breaths before he could continue the conversation.

"Yeah, I don't think Jonathan is going to give up that easily either. But, hopefully, we're wrong."

"I hope so. Paisley has been through enough." Everly took the bottle of beer he'd just pulled out of the cooler from him. "I can cover for my sister. You need to clean up the kitchen and get out of here. Shane told me you still put in a full day's work at the ranch—even on the days you're working here."

"Ranch work has never been work for me. And I'd probably be here at night even if I wasn't working."

"But you wouldn't be slaving away in a kitchen. You'd be dancing the night away with some pretty cowgirl."

"I still have Fridays and Saturdays to dance with pretty cowgirls." It was too bad there was only one woman he wanted to dance with. And the chances of that happening were slim to none.

Unaware of his thoughts about her sister, Everly smiled. "Well, I appreciate you helping me out while Gretchen is on maternity leave. I know you love cowboying much more than you love cooking."

He couldn't argue the point. Cowboying was in his blood and always had been. Until he'd arrived at the Kingman Ranch, he hadn't understood how a boy who had grown up with a carpenter stepdaddy and a mama who was fearful of horses loved them so much. Now it all made sense.

The phone rang and Everly answered it. By the lovesick look on her face, Hayden figured it was Chance. Her next words confirmed it.

"I love it when you talk dirty, Preach. But we're going to have to wait to try that out until I get home. And you better not go to sleep before I get there."

After she hung up, she still looked lovesick. Hayden hoped one day he'd make a woman look like that. If he did find that woman, he hoped some nice guy would help him out and get her home to him sooner.

"Why don't you leave early tonight?" he said. "I'll close up."

"Absolutely not. You can't close the bar at one and get up at six."

"I've gone to bed much later. Believe me." He took the beer bottle from her and winked. "And if it can't be me, I want someone to have a Valentine's night to remember."

CHAPTER THREE

"YOU DON'T HAVE to stay. I can close up just fine on my own."

Hayden's husky voice had Paisley almost dropping the dirty glass she'd been about to put in the dishwasher. She'd thought he was in the kitchen cleaning up. Obviously not.

She continued loading the dishwasher, her gaze on anything but the man standing at the end of the bar. "I told Everly I would help you and I'm going to help you."

There was a long pause. "Okay, then. I'll do the mopping."

She waited until she heard the clicks of his bootheels heading away from her before she lifted her gaze and watched as he effortlessly flipped the chairs up on the tables. While she felt exhausted, he moved like he still had plenty of energy. As she turned on the dishwasher and then started polishing glass and bottle rings off the bar top, she continued to covertly watch him.

He was an expert at mopping as much as he seemed to be an expert at everything else. He worked his way from one corner of the bar to the other in long sideways strokes that caused his back muscles to flex and release. Paisley tried to remember if she had ever watched a man mop before and couldn't come up with one memory. Mopping had been her mother's job and there were always housekeepers at the large house she'd lived in with Jonathan and his parents. Which probably explained a lot. As the spoiled only child of a judge and doting socialite mother, Jonathan had never felt like he needed to clean up any of his messes.

And he'd certainly made a mess of Paisley.

She had thought leaving him would fix everything. That once she was away from his abusive control, her life would fall into place and she'd be happy. But that hadn't happened. She didn't feel happy. She felt lost. Like a puppet without her puppeteer. She didn't know where to go from here. Or even who she was. The only thing she clung to was being a good mother to Henry. And, now, she wasn't even that.

Mean mama.

Henry's words had hurt . . . as had him siding with a man he'd only known for a few months. Since she couldn't blame a five-year-old, she blamed Hayden. And with good reason. It was Hayden's fault Henry had snuck out and crossed a busy street. Maybe not directly, but indirectly. Henry was an impressionable child who never had a strong male role model. Jonathan had never wanted a child and from the day Henry was born had resented him taking Paisley's attention. Because she hadn't wanted him taking his anger out on Henry, she hadn't pushed him to be a parent. Or maybe she'd just liked having her son all to herself.

She and Henry had been a team. The dynamic duo.

Until now.

Now Henry had other people in his life. While Paisley was glad her son had so many people to count on, she didn't want him getting girl advice from a rodeo bum who probably had a woman in every city he'd been in.

After she had taken Henry back to Hester's, she'd gotten the truth about why Henry had snuck out. Once again, she'd felt hurt Henry hadn't told her about the girl he liked. It had been bad enough that he'd shared the information with Everly. But Hayden? A man he barely knew? And how dare that man think he had the right to give love advice to her five-year-old son? According to Everly, Hayden had never been in love. Or even in a serious relationship. And yet, he thought he could butt his nose in where it didn't belong?

When Hayden finished mopping and headed to the kitchen with the bucket and mop, she stopped him.

"I don't want you giving my son advice about girls anymore."

Hayden halted in his tracks and turned to her. After a nerve-racking amount of time where he only stared at her, he nodded. "You're right. Not my business."

"And it's not your business to fill Henry's head

full of cowboy stories or glamorize the lifestyle so all he can talk about is becoming a cowboy and riding horses. Henry just turned five. That's way too young to be on a horse."

He set down the bucket and leaned on the mop. "Well, ma'am, I guess that depends on the horse and the teacher. My daddy taught me when I was about Henry's age." A smile tugged at the corners of his wide mouth. "But only after I bugged him every day for months. Like you, my mama was against it. But Jimmy finally convinced her that he wouldn't let anything happen to me." His smile won out. He had one of those smiles that took over his entire face, creasing his cheeks and crinkling the corners of his eyes. "And he didn't. He bought me a sweet mare named Rosie and walked me around the paddock for weeks before he let me take the reins." He shook his head. "I don't think I've ever felt so proud in all my life." He glanced at her and his smile faded. "But I understand why you don't want Henry to ride. And I won't talk about cowboying again. Although I don't think I can stop him from asking about it."

"No, I don't expect that you can. He's much too taken with you, and I don't have a clue why." Once the words were out of her mouth, she wanted them back. She had never been so rude in her life and she quickly apologized. "I'm sorry. I shouldn't have said that."

"That's okay. The truth is the truth. And I'm not exactly a good role model for a kid." He paused. "But I understand why Henry needs one."

Paisley understood too. But she wasn't about to go into the details of her marriage. "Yes, well, he has a lot of other male role models in his life. Chance and his brother, Shane. And all the Kingmans."

An expression crossed Hayden's face. "Yes, the Kingmans. Of course, they'd be the best role models." He picked up the bucket and pushed his way into the kitchen.

When he was gone, Paisley puzzled over his reaction. Was Hayden jealous of the Kingmans? It made sense. The Kingmans were successful ranchers who ran one of the biggest ranch businesses in Texas. The five siblings and their spouses lived in an actual castle and were pretty much considered royalty by the townsfolk.

They did seem to have storybook lives.

The oldest brother, Stetson, had married a famous children's book author and he and Lily had just had a son a few months earlier. Then there was Adeline, who was married to the ranch foreman, Gage Reardon. Addie and Gage had also had a son the year before. Next came Wolfe, who owned the bar and was married to Gretchen. Wolfe and Gretchen's daughter, Maribelle, had been born right after Thanksgiving. Delaney was the youngest girl in the family. She had married Chance's twin brother, Shane, and they were expecting their first child. And finally there was Buck who had married Hester's granddaughter, Mystic. Mystic was pregnant as well.

All the Kingmans claimed to have found love

and appeared to be living happily ever after . . . appeared to be.

Paisley knew that appearances could be deceiving.

Everyone in her small town of Mesaville had thought she had a storybook life. She'd grown up in a picture-perfect two-story house with a white picket fence, manicured lawns, and a wide porch with a quaint swing her father kept pristinely painted. She and Everly had rooms most little girls dream about. Canopy beds, and frilly curtains, and shelves filled with toys and dolls. Her parents were the nice neighbors who took soup to people who were sick, helped them do odd jobs, and brought the best dishes to Christmas parties and potlucks.

But it was all for show.

Beneath their spotless, starched clothes and fake smiles, her parents were as controlling as Jonathan. They hadn't used physical abuse, but the emotional bruises they'd left had harmed Paisley and Everly just as much . . . if not more. They had expected their daughters to be perfect little angels. To never get dirty. To never speak unless spoken to. To never talk back. To be what people expected southern young ladies to be. To hide their true thoughts and emotions behind a pleasant smile and an "I'm just fine, thank you. How are you?"

Paisley had learned the lessons her parents had taught too well. So much so that she didn't even know what her true thoughts and desires were. She felt like a blank chalkboard waiting for someone to write on.

Her depressing thoughts made her feel even more exhausted and she quickly finished polishing the bar and started closing down the register. She had just locked all the cash and credit card receipts in the safe when she heard the sound of breaking glass come through the door of the kitchen—shortly followed by Hayden's angry cursing.

Paisley's body froze and fear shot through her like pure adrenaline injected straight into her veins. Her first thought was to leave . . . quickly. And she might have done just that if she hadn't heard another crash. This time, it wasn't just glass. This time, it was a loud thump of something heavy falling. On shaky legs, she moved to the kitchen door and pushed it open a crack. Her eyes widened when she saw Hayden lying on the floor next to the prep counter with blood splattered on the front of his shirt.

Fear for herself took a back seat to fear for Hayden. She pushed through the door and hurried over to him. "Hayden!" She knelt next to him. Just as she placed two fingers on his neck to feel for his pulse, his eyes fluttered open and he blinked in confusion.

"What happened?"

She removed her hand from his neck. "I don't know. I heard the sound of breaking glass, followed by a loud crash, and I came in to find you lying on the floor. Are you okay?"

He sat up and nodded. "Yeah, I just broke a

plate and cut my hand." He lifted his hand. Blood dripped off a cut on his palm. When he saw it, his face lost all color and his eyes rolled back in his head.

Paisley grabbed the front of his shirt before he fell over. She lowered him carefully, then reached up and got a dish towel from the counter. By the time she had it wrapped around his hand, Hayden was coming to again. He started to get up, but she pushed him back down.

"No, sir. You stay right there and don't look." She lifted the towel to examine the wound on his palm. It was oozing blood, but not enough to warrant an emergency room visit.

"I think you'll be okay." She rewrapped his hand. "Stay put and breathe while I get something to clean and bandage your cut." She got the first aid kit that was kept under the bar for emergencies. When she came back to the kitchen, she found Hayden sitting on a stool at the prep counter looking sheepish.

"I have a thing with my own blood."

"I noticed." She set the first aid kit on the counter and opened it. Once she selected the right-sized bandage and tore open an antiseptic wipe, she picked up Hayden's hand and removed the towel. "This might sting." If it did, Hayden didn't make a sound as she cleaned the cut. Once most of the blood was gone, she couldn't help noticing all the calluses on his palm. "Don't you wear gloves?" When he didn't reply, she glanced up to find his deep blue eyes pinned on her. His face was no longer pale. In fact, his cheeks were flushed. "Are you okay? You aren't going to faint again, are you?" She pressed her fingers to his wrist. "Your pulse is a little rapid."

He looked away and cleared his throat. "No. I'm good."

She went back to cleaning the wound. For some reason—the late hour, her exhaustion, or possibly finding a chink in a tough rodeo cowboy's armor—a giggle escaped her mouth. Then another. Until she was out-and-out laughing. She couldn't remember the last time she'd laughed so hard. She couldn't seem to stop. It had to be exhaustion. With all her fears of the future, she hadn't been sleeping well, and working nights and waking up early to get Henry ready for school didn't help.

"So you think it's funny, do you?" Hayden said. Worried she'd made him angry, she sobered and glanced up. But he wasn't angry. He had a big grin on his face and his eyes twinkled merrily. "Well, it is. Damn funny. I can birth a foal or a calf, clean up piles of horse poop—and every other kind of animal excrement—but I can't handle the sight of my own blood."

"It's not that strange. When I was in nursing school, I ran into a lot of patients who couldn't handle the sight of their own blood."

His head tipped. "You're a nurse?"

She returned her attention to putting antibiotic ointment on his cut. "I have a degree in nursing, but I never got licensed or worked as a nurse."

"Why not?"

"I got married."

"So?"

"I wanted to focus on being a wife." The lie came easily. It was the one she told when anyone asked her why she had given up a career she had worked so hard for and been so excited about. Most of the people in her town easily accepted the lie. Who would want to work when they were marrying the son of the wealthiest and most prestigious family in town?

She swallowed down the lump that had formed in the back of her throat and opened the bandage. When it was sealed securely around the cut, she drew back. "There. That should do it." She lifted her gaze and discovered Hayden frowning. "Did I hurt you?"

The frown eased. "No. You have a gentle touch. I can see you being a good nurse. Why don't you take it back up?"

She started collecting the wrappers. "Because it's been too long. I'd have to go back to school in order to pass the licensing tests and I don't have the time or the money."

"I'm sure Everly would make sure you have the time. And you aren't getting a settlement?"

"Not that it's any of your business, but no. I don't want anything from Jonathan. Except for him to leave me and Henry alone. And I refuse to make my sister—who just got married—work harder because I want to go back to school."

"I'm sure she wouldn't mind. That's what family is for. To help you out when you need it. And colleges have online courses. They might even offer financial assistance." He hesitated. "Do you really think Jonathan will leave you alone just because you don't take what's rightfully yours?"

She refused to answer. Maybe if she didn't voice her greatest fear, it wouldn't become a reality.

She got up from the stool. "I need to get home." She picked up the first aid kit and carried it back to the bar. After she checked to make sure she'd locked the safe, she grabbed her purse from under the bar and started turning off the lights. When she was finished, Hayden came out of the kitchen. Since it was unnerving to be with him alone in the dark bar, she didn't waste any time heading for the door.

Everly had left her the key. Once outside, she waited for Hayden so she could lock the door. It had been a cold, wet winter. Cursed had gotten a light dusting of snow three times thus far. Tonight, the sky was clear, but it was freezing. As she locked the door, she wished she'd brought her coat.

"Well, good night," she said as she headed for the street. She startled when Hayden followed her and draped his jacket over her shoulders. "I don't—"

He cut her off. "I know you don't need anything from me, Paisley. But my mama would tan my hide if I didn't offer a lady my coat when she was cold. Or walk her home when it was dark. Now you wouldn't want all my mama's lessons to be wasted, would you?"

She started to argue, but the warmth of his insulated jacket had her closing her mouth. When they reached the street, she went to cross, but

Hayden's words stopped her. "Crossing without looking both ways? Shame on you, Ms. Stanford."

She shot him an annoyed look before she crossed.

The house Hester lived in was a brand-new, two-story farmhouse with a big porch in front and a neon sign in the window. *Fortunetelling and Palm Reading.* The sign had made Paisley more than a little leery about moving into the house. But once she'd met Hester, those fears had evaporated. A kinder hearted person Paisley had never met in her life. Hester was the type of strong, independent woman Paisley wished she could be. She hadn't just offered Paisley and Henry a place to live, but she'd also become like a grandmother to Henry and a comforting mother figure to Paisley.

Yes, there were strange things about her—like Hester's ability to read Paisley's thoughts—but Paisley figured that had more to do with experience and wisdom than actual psychic ability.

When they reached the porch steps, Paisley took off Hayden's jacket and held it out to him. "Thank you."

"Thank you for bandaging me up." He took the jacket and their fingers accidentally brushed. The current of heat that arched between them took Paisley completely by surprise. She had touched his hand back at the bar and felt nothing. Now, suddenly, she felt like a lit match. And maybe it had nothing to do with the touch. Maybe it had to do with how close he stood to her and the intensity of his gaze beneath the brim of his cowboy hat. In the kitchen when he had moved toward her, she had stepped back. Now, suddenly, she wanted to step closer. She wanted to be enfolded in his arms and pressed against his hard chest. She wanted to absorb the heat and strength of his body and, for just a second, feel like everything was going to be okay.

But she had made the mistake of leaning on a man before and look where that had gotten her.

So instead of stepping closer, she turned and fled.

CHAPTER FOUR

HAYDEN HAD HEARD stories about Buckinghorse Palace long before he arrived at the Kingman Ranch. As a young kid, he had never dreaded bedtime because that was when his mother would fill his head with stories about a cowboy castle with stone turrets that reached the sky, solid oak doors big enough for a giant to fit through, and wide balconies perfect for beautiful princesses to call down to their cowboy princes.

As an adult, Hayden thought his mother had grossly elaborated the stories to entertain her son.

She hadn't.

The castle did have turrets that reached well into the blue Texas sky. The oak doors were big enough for a giant, or at least a giant of a man, to fit through, and the balconies were perfect for beautiful princesses to call down from.

One was doing so right now.

"Gage!"

Gage Reardon stopped heading toward Hayden and turned back to the castle. Adeline stood on the second-floor balcony holding a chubby-cheeked Danny on her hip. The expression on Gage's face as he looked up at his wife and son was pure adoration. As was Adeline's as she looked down at her husband. Danny seemed busy tugging on his mama's long blond hair. It reminded Hayden of Paisley's, but lighter. Adeline's was more like moonlight while Paisley's was more like rays of brilliant sunshine.

"Don't forget I have a Cursed Ladies' Auxiliary meeting this afternoon," Adeline said. "But if you're busy, I'm sure Wolfe can watch Danny since he's already watching Maribelle."

"No," Gage said. "I can do it. I'm planning on taking Danny over to the refuge barn to see Del's goats." His voice changed to baby talk, which was a little disconcerting when Gage was a badass cowboy who had once been an even bigger badass Marine. "Isn't that wight, Dano? You want to go see Sleepy, Sneezy, Gwumpy, Bashful, Happy, Doc, and Dopey with your daddy? Do ya, my big boy?"

Danny finally stopped playing with Adeline's hair and noticed his daddy. His fat legs started pumping and his fists waving as he squealed.

Gage grinned like any proud papa. "Daddy loves you too."

Adeline smiled down at her husband. "And we love you."

Gage blew her a kiss and she blew one back. Feeling extremely uncomfortable at being a witness to what should be a private moment, Hayden decided whatever Gage had wanted to see him about could wait. But when he turned to leave, Gage stopped him.

"Hayden! Where are you going? I wanted to talk with you."

He turned back around. "I thought I'd give you and Mrs. Reardon some privacy to say goodbye."

"Hayden," Adeline called down. "How many times do I have to tell you? Any man willing to keep my son occupied during his fussy time can call me Adeline."

"Sorry, ma'am . . . I mean Adeline."

She smiled. "You're forgiven. Y'all have a good morning now." She turned with Danny and swept through the French doors.

Gage continued to stare at the balcony with a lovesick smile on his face. At one time, Hayden wouldn't have understood how a man could make such a fool of himself over a woman. He understood now. Last night, he'd felt like a puddle of lovesick pudding when Paisley had been doctoring his hand. Her gentle touch had taken all thoughts from his head, except for one. Kissing her. Later, when they had been standing in front of Hester's house and their fingers had brushed, he'd been about to.

And Paisley had known it.

She had raced into the house like a cat with its tail on fire. If that didn't tell him everything he needed to know, he was a damn fool. Paisley wasn't interested in him. And rightly so. She was just getting out of an abusive relationship and had other things on her mind than a lovesick cowboy who had let his heart get away from him.

Refocusing on the present moment, he cleared

his throat. "So what did you want to talk to me about, Gage?"

Gage turned to him. "Stetson wanted me to go to Dallas with him to drop off one of our mares for breeding. But as you heard, Adeline has a ladies' meeting in town and Stet and I won't be back in time for me to watch Danny. So I thought you could go with Stet."

Being stuck in the car with the oldest Kingman for more than four hours round trip was not Hayden's idea of a good time. While he got along just fine with the rest of the Kingmans, he did not get along with Stetson. In fact, he didn't like the man at all. As far as Hayden was concerned, Stetson was a control freak who thought he was in charge of everything and everyone on the ranch.

Stetson didn't seem to like Hayden either. Whenever they were in the same vicinity, Hayden always caught Stetson watching him. And not with a friendly expression. In fact, Hayden was pretty sure Stetson would have already let him go if Hayden wasn't helping at the bar so Gretchen and Wolfe could stay home with their new daughter. While Stetson was controlling, he always put his family's needs before his own.

"Thanks," Hayden said. "But I'll have to pass. I have a lot to get done here today before I head to Nasty Jack's."

Suddenly, the doting husband and father was gone, replaced by the stern ranch foreman. "It wasn't a question, Hayden."

Hayden pinned on a smile. "Then I'd love to."

Thirty minutes later, Hayden showed up at the house with the mare loaded in the horse trailer hitched to his truck and found Stetson waiting out front. He and Stetson were less than a year apart in age and had the same build. Although Hayden was positive if they were measured, he'd be taller. Their hair was the same dark brown. Their jaws pronounced. Their foreheads too high. But their personalities weren't alike. Not alike at all.

Stetson was a grumpy asshole.

"Like I told Gage, I don't need company," he said as soon as Hayden got out of the truck.

Hayden shrugged and handed Stetson his keys. "Yes, sir." He started to head to the stables, but Stetson's words stopped him.

"Where are you going? We need to head out if we want to make it back for your shift at Nasty's."

Hayden rolled his eyes before he turned and got in the passenger side of his truck. For the first ten minutes of driving, there was complete silence. Hayden had never liked silence. Probably because, as an only child, he'd grown up with way too much of it. When he couldn't take a second more, he turned on the radio. Stetson shot him an annoyed look, but didn't say a word.

Most of the stations he'd programmed in played old country and western music: Hank Williams, George Jones, Tammy Wynette, and Loretta Lynn. His stepdaddy loved all the country singers of the fifties and sixties and had played them so much Hayden learned to love them too. When a Marty Robbins song came on, Hayden couldn't help singing along. He was more than a little shocked when Stetson joined in. They both had deep baritone voices that worked nicely with the song about falling in love with a Mexican girl.

When the song was over, Hayden glanced at Stetson. "You like Marty?"

Stetson shrugged. "He was one of my grand-daddy's favorite singers. I don't remember a lot about King, but I remember his love of country and western music." A rare smile came over his face. "He'd sing his favorite songs to the cattle when he took me herding with him. I thought he was like the Pied Piper and got the cows to do what he wanted just by singing."

"I heard your granddaddy was a damned good cowboy. Of course, he had to be to build a ranch like yours."

"He was one of the best cowboys I've ever known. It wasn't just his riding and roping skills. He had a way with animals. Something that can't be taught. It's either in you or it's not. It was in King." Stetson hesitated. "It's too bad he wasn't as good with people."

Hayden looked back at the highway and tried to hide his interest. "I heard that too."

Stetson snorted. "It's no secret my grandfather was an arrogant, controlling man who expected everyone to bend to his will . . . or be snapped in two."

"And your father? Did he bend?"

There was a long stretch of silence before Stetson spoke. "He tried to. But in the end, he just ended up broken. He felt like he could never fill

King's big boots, which probably explains why he never tried. He didn't care about the family business. He rarely showed up at the stables or on the range. The ranch was just his home. It was never his passion."

"And what was his passion?" he asked, even though he already knew the answer.

Stetson's hands visibly tightened on the steering wheel. "Women. My daddy loved women."

Hayden's own hands tightened into fists as he turned away. Outside the window, a herd of Black Angus cattle grazed. Cattle he had helped Wolfe, Buck, and Stetson herd to that very spot not more than a few days earlier. Douglas Kingman might not have had a passion for ranching, but his sons did.

All his sons.

A Conway Twitty song came on and Stetson started to sing along.

Hayden joined in.

The ranch they were leaving the mare at was located right outside of Dallas. It was a pretty ranch with a white slat fence, extensive and well cared-for stables, and a big brick house with a five-car garage. The owner, Dale White, was a barrel of a man with a loud, booming voice and overbearing personality. As he showed them around, Hayden could tell he was quite proud of his ranch and wanted to hear compliments. He didn't get them. As a ranch hand, Hayden didn't feel like it was his place and Stetson wasn't a complimenting kind of guy.

At least, he wasn't until they got to the stables.

Then Stetson didn't hesitate to compliment Dale on his horses. He did have some fine-looking thoroughbreds. The best-looking one was the stud Stetson had chosen. Royal Duke was sleek and muscled, but Hayden had learned that looks could be deceiving. The stallion might be a beauty, but something wasn't right with the horse. When he was led out of the stables, he seemed too docile. Especially when an in-heat mare was in the trailer not more than twelve feet away. Most studs would be restless and yanking at the reins to get to their woman. This horse just stood there with his head drooping.

While Stetson and the owner spoke about breeding terms, Hayden walked over and examined the stallion. He ran a hand along the horse's back and it came away wet with sweat.

"This horse just been exercised?" Hayden asked the ranch hand holding the reins.

The ranch hand kept his eyes lowered and shook his head. "No, sir."

Hayden lifted the horse's head. "Hey, boy. You sure are pretty." The horse looked back at him with sleepy eyes and a relaxed lower lip. "And you sure are drugged."

The ranch hand's eyes shot to Hayden, then over to his owner, who cut off his conversation with Stetson and hurried over. "Is there a problem?"

Hayden looked at Stetson. "This horse has been drugged. And the only reason to drug a horse is because you don't want them showing their bad traits."

Stetson turned to the owner. "You drugged him?"

Dale puffed his chest out. "Just what are you accusing me of?"

Stetson ignored the question and looked at the ranch hand. "Did you drug this horse?"

The ranch hand swallowed hard. "He's a little high strung so Mr. White thought we should give him something to calm him down."

Stetson shot Dale a look Hayden wouldn't want to be on the receiving end of. "Funny, but you didn't mention him being high strung when we talked on the phone. In fact, you said he had a calm disposition." Before the man could reply, Stetson continued. "The deal is off. Not because your stallion is high strung, but because his owner is a liar. I don't deal with liars. Or people who drug animals." He looked at Hayden. "Let's go."

"Yes, sir."

Once they were in the truck, Stetson released his anger. "Stupid asshole drugging an animal to hide his own lies! If I hadn't given Lily my word that I'd tone down my temper, I would have given that fool more than a few choice words."

"Mrs. Kingman wouldn't find out from me," Hayden said. "You want to go back? I'll hold off the ranch hands."

Stetson glanced at him and a smile broke over his face. It was the first time he'd smiled at Hayden. For some reason, Hayden felt like he'd accomplished something. "Thanks, but I have other ways to deal with assholes. I'm going to make sure every rancher in Texas knows what kind of breeder Dale White is."

Hayden figured that was worse than punching the guy. The Kingmans had clout in Texas. When Stetson spoke, most people listened. Dale would probably be out of the breeding business within a year. Which might work in Hayden's favor. He didn't mind high-strung horses. Maybe he'd be able to work a deal with the owner to buy the stallion and a few other horses . . . long distance, of course. Dale wouldn't be willing to make a deal with the man who had pointed out his deception.

On the drive back to the Kingman Ranch, Stetson was much more talkative. And so was Hayden. They talked about horses and cattle, then moved on to football. While talking about the Dallas Cowboys' pathetic efforts in the play-offs, Hayden mentioned playing defensive end in high school. Considering his size, Hayden figured Stetson had played a little football in his life and was surprised when he hadn't.

"I would've liked to play," Stetson said. "But I was too busy with the ranch and taking care of my younger siblings to play sports."

Hayden glanced over at him. He knew Stetson's mother had died when he was young, but his father hadn't died until Stetson was almost out of college. "Where was your daddy?"

"Daddy felt the same way about parenting as he did about running the ranch. He preferred someone else did the job."

Hayden now understood why Stetson was so

controlling. He'd had to be. "Sounds like you had the responsibility of your family from an early age. Did you ever resent it?"

Stetson nodded. "And sometimes I still do."

"Your siblings are grown now, you know? The responsibility of running the ranch and keeping your family together doesn't have to be all yours."

"I know. But it's hard to let go and stop being the big brother in charge." He glanced at Hayden. "Where do you fall in your family?"

Hayden stared out at the highway. "I'm an only child. Which makes me fall nowhere ... nowhere, at all."

CHAPTER FIVE

"**H**ENRY HIT SOMEONE?" Paisley stared at Henry's preschool teacher in stunned disbelief.

Miss Phelps nodded. "I was as surprised as you. Henry might be talkative, but he's never been aggressive with the other children. In fact, he's usually helpful and kind. And I wouldn't have believed it if I hadn't witnessed him punching Brendan with my own two eyes."

Punching? Paisley glanced over at Henry, who was sitting on the floor in the Lego section of the classroom snapping the small plastic pieces together. When he glanced up and saw her and Miss Phelps looking at him, his guilty expression confirmed what Miss Phelps had just told her.

Paisley suddenly felt like she was going to be sick. She had known Henry was in trouble when Miss Phelps had asked her to stay until the rest of the children had left so they could talk. But Paisley had thought it would be about something simple like Henry hadn't gotten his schoolwork done or he talked too much during class time.

She hadn't thought it was because her son had become violent.

Some of her anxiety must have shown because Miss Phelps reached out and patted her shoulder.

"It's nothing to get upset about, Mrs. Stanford. This happens quite often at this age. Children are still figuring out how to deal with their emotions. When they can't find words for their anger, hitting seems to be the next best thing. I had a long talk with Henry about using words instead of fists and I don't think this will happen again."

If Paisley hadn't just gotten out of an abusive situation, she might have been able to accept Miss Phelps's reassurance that this was just normal five-year-old behavior. But after living with an abusive husband, she couldn't help worrying that there was more to it. Was there such a thing as a violent gene? Or had Henry seen something he shouldn't have? She had tried so hard to use excuses for her bruises, but Henry was a smart kid. Had he figured things out and thought hitting was okay?

Swallowing down the bile that had risen to the back of her throat, she forced a smile. "Well, thank you, Miss Phelps, for letting me know. I'll make sure Henry is appropriately disciplined for his actions. Is the little boy he hit okay?"

"Brendan is fine. An hour after it happened, he and Henry were playing Legos together. Children don't hold grudges. But I felt like it was something you needed to know so you can reinforce the severity of the situation at home."

Paisley nodded and thanked the teacher again before she walked over to where Henry was playing. "Clean up, Henry. It's time to go." At home, he usually tried to talk his way out of cleaning up his toys. Today, he quickly placed all the Legos he'd gotten out back in the colorful plastic bins before he stood and walked over to get his coat and backpack off his hook.

He didn't say anything until he was buckled in his booster seat. "I'm sorry, Mama. But let me 'splain."

She shook her head. "There is no good explanation for what you did, Henry James. It was wrong. Terribly wrong." Her voice shook with all the emotions clamoring around inside her. She realized she needed to calm down before she talked with Henry about what happened. "But we'll talk about this later."

When they got to the Malones' house, they found Hester sitting on the sofa in the living room. Her tarot cards were spread out on the coffee table in front of her and Wish, Mystic's large black cat, was sleeping next to her.

"Guess what, Hessy?" Henry flopped down on the sofa and pulled the sleeping cat into his arms. "I'm in big trouble."

Hester lifted her eyebrows. While her long hair was silver, her eyebrows were jet black. "Well, I'm sorry to hear that. I hope you're not in so much trouble that you can't have the peanut butter cookies I put out for your snack."

Henry sent Paisley a pleading look. "Can I, Mama? I lobe peanut butter cookies."

Paisley nodded. "You can have a snack, but there will be no afternoon cartoons."

"Aw-w-w." He got up and headed for the kitchen with Wish draped over his shoulder.

When he was gone, Hester set down the tarot cards she held in her hand and picked up the teapot sitting on the tray and poured two cups. "Mystic was supposed to take a break from working in her salon and come have tea, but I saw Buck's truck pull in a few minutes ago so I figure she has better things to do on her break than sip tea with her grandmother." She picked up a teacup and held it out. "Which works out since you look like you could use a cup."

There was something soothing about Hester's tea. After just a few sips, Paisley's stomach settled and she was able to speak without her voice shaking.

"Henry hit a boy at school."

Hester leaned back on the sofa and studied her with her piercing violet eyes. "And you're worried he got his father's violent nature."

Tears pricked Paisley's eyes, but she blinked them back. "I know it's silly, but I can't seem to help it. And I'm not worried he got Jonathan's nature as much as I'm worried it was something we taught him. I tried so hard to hide the abuse from Henry, but what if Jonathan and I taught him hitting is okay?"

"You?"

She nodded. "I'm just as responsible as Jonathan. I allowed the abuse to keep happening. And that's almost worse. I taught Henry that his mother is a weak person who couldn't stand up for herself or her son."

Hester set down her cup. "You did what you thought was best at the time to keep your son safe, Paisley. When things got bad, you *were* strong enough to leave. You proved it. Not only to Henry, but to yourself. Now you need to stop worrying and overthinking everything. All kids hit from time to time. I don't think it had to do with having his father's traits or seeing something he shouldn't have. Did you ask him why he hit Brendan?"

"No. I was too upset."

"I can see that." Hester studied her. "And are you sure it just has to do with Henry? Or is something else bothering you? You've seemed jumpy all day."

Hester was right. Paisley had been jumpy all day. There was a good reason. "Kitty said she had a package for me at the post office and she'd deliver it today. She didn't come while I was gone, did she?"

"No, and I assume what's in this package is what has you so nervous."

She nodded as she set her teacup down. "I'm pretty sure it's the divorce papers. My lawyer said she'd sent them to Jonathan's lawyers for him to sign. I thought I'd be relieved the nightmare is over. But all I feel is . . ."

"Scared."

She sighed. "It's pathetic, isn't it? I felt more comfortable in a life where I was being con trolled and abused than I do in a life where I now have control."

Hester patted Paisley's knee. "It's not pathetic. It makes perfect sense. Control can be scary. It's like the first time you get behind the wheel of a car. You aren't a passenger anymore. You're the driver. If you make a mistake and get in an accident, it's totally on you. If you have a little boy sitting in the car with you, it's even scarier. You drive slow and keep your foot over the brake, looking around for anything that could jump in your way. It will take time to get over your fears. Time to trust yourself and your abilities to navigate life and get you and Henry safely through it."

Hester's eyes held compassion. "It's twice as hard for a woman who has spent most of her life doing what other people expected her to do. But if you want to move forward, Paisley, you'll have to put aside your fears and have the courage to press on the gas."

The tears that had only threatened suddenly rolled down Paisley's cheeks. "What if I don't have enough courage, Hessy? What if I not only mess up my life, but Henry's?"

Hester scooted closer and pulled Paisley into her arms. "You have enough courage. It takes courage to survive what you did. You just need to believe in the strong woman you are. When I look at you, I see a fierce mama lion. A lion who needs to take hold of her power and start fighting for what she wants."

The door opened and Mystic stepped in.

"Sorry, I'm late, Hess—" She cut off when she saw Paisley. "Hi, Paisley." Her violet eyes that were identical to her grandmother's grew concerned. "Is everything okay?"

Paisley started to say everything was just fine like her parents had taught her. But instead she did something she had never done before. She told the truth.

"No," she said. "Everything isn't okay. I'm one hot mess."

It wasn't until much later that Paisley felt calm enough to talk with Henry about what had happened at school. After getting ready for work, she searched him out and found him in the backyard playing in the dirt with the Tonka trucks she had given him for his recent birthday. When he saw her, the smile he had on his face turned into a frown. A frown she had seen often in the last few months. She hated that he was no longer happy to see her, but it was her own fault. She'd been too preoccupied with keeping herself afloat to pay much attention to her son.

Rather than make the frown worse by interrogating him, she sat down on the ground and started playing. She dug up dirt with a backhoe and piled it high so he could scoop it into the bucket of the front loader and dump it in the bed of the big yellow dump truck.

After a few minutes of moving dirt, he finally spoke. "Are you still mad at me, Mama?"

She stopped digging. "I was never mad at you, Henry. I was just surprised you would want to hit someone."

"I didn't mean to hit Brendan, but when he started saying Brooklyn Ann was his girlfriend and not mine, I got mad."

"Getting angry is no reason to hit. Violence is never the solution. Never."

Henry scrunched his face. "Neber? But what if a bad guy breaks into Hester's house and tries to hurt you and Hessy?" It had actually happened. Jonathan had broken into Hester's after Paisley had left him. Thankfully, Henry had been at the church rehearsing for the Christmas musical and hadn't witnessed his father choking her . . . or being handcuffed by the sheriff. But had he overheard her talking to Everly about that night? Not wanting to lie, she didn't deny it could happen.

"Then I would call the sheriff."

"But what if the bad guy ties you up before you can and I'm the only one who can sabe you? I might habe to hit someone then. I might habe to pick up a pan and hit them right ober the head like Jerry does to Tom in that cartoon."

Obviously, she needed to monitor more closely the cartoons Henry was watching. "Well, thank you for wanting to protect me. But we're not talking about what could happen. We're talking about you hitting Brendan just because he likes the same little girl you do."

"But sometimes a man has to stand his ground and not let people get the best of him. And that's what I was doing with Brendan when he said that Brooklyn Ann was his girlfriend, not mine. I was standing my ground just like Hay told me to."

Paisley stared at her son. "Like Hayden told you to? He told you to hit a little boy?"

Henry must have heard the anger in her voice because his eyes got big and he shook his head. "No-o-o."

It was obvious he was lying to save Hayden. Which made Paisley even angrier. "Well, Hayden was wrong. Punching is not the way to solve a problem. And I don't want you hanging around Hayden anymore. He's a bad influence."

Henry stared at her. "But I lobe Hay. He's a cowboy. And I want to be just like him when I grow up."

"Believe me, you don't want to be like Hayden when you grow up. He's nothing but a saddle tramp who probably doesn't have two dimes to rub together."

"Yes, he does!" Henry jumped to his feet. "He let me count the change in his pocket and he has fibe dimes and two quarters and seben pennies. And he's not a saddle tramp. He's a cowboy. The best cowboy eber. And if you don't let me see him, I'll go libe with Daddy. He'll let me see Hay!"

Talk about being punched. Henry's words felt like a hard punch in the stomach. She got to her feet and tried to keep her hurt from showing. "You aren't living with your father. And you aren't hanging around Hayden anymore either. Now, pick up your trucks and let's go inside. I need to get to work."

Henry glared at her. "No!" He turned and raced off.

Paisley sighed and picked up his trucks. She should make him take them back to the porch, but she had to be at work. And honestly, she was too tired to argue with him. She figured he had run into the house to tell Hester how mean his mama was. But when she came around the corner of the house, she saw him headed for the main street. Usually there was very little traffic, but today a semi was coming down the street much faster than the speed limit. Her heart plummeted to her feet and she dropped the trucks and ran faster than she had ever run in her life.

"Henry! Stop right now!"

But he didn't listen. Nor did he look both ways before he charged across the street. There was a squeal of semi brakes. If Henry had kept running, everything would have been fine. But, at the sound of the squealing brakes, Henry froze in the middle of the street.

"No!" Paisley screamed in a voice that didn't sound like her own. Before her entire world could end, Hayden appeared out of nowhere and scooped Henry up in his arms and raced across the street just as the semi slid to a stop in the exact spot Henry had been standing.

As Paisley pressed a hand to her chest and whispered a prayer of thanks, the trucker rolled down his window and cussed at Hayden for being a piss-poor father and not watching his son. Hayden offered an apology before he started yelling at Henry.

"What were you thinking? Didn't your mama tell you not to cross that street without an adult?

Don't you ever—and I mean ever—do it again or I'll paddle your butt myself. Do you hear me, Henry?"

His threat had Paisley overcoming her fear of almost losing her son and she charged over to take Henry from Hayden. "You won't ever lay a hand on my son. Do you hear me? Ever."

Hayden didn't back down. In fact, he stepped closer. "Then you need to. Because whatever discipline you gave him the other night for sneaking out and crossing the street alone obviously didn't work."

Setting Henry down, she got in Hayden's face. "How I discipline my son is my business. I don't need anyone's advice or interference."

"If I hadn't interfered, your son would've been flattened by a thirty-thousand-pound truck. I figure that gives me the right to state my mind."

That took all the wind out of her sails. Just the thought of Henry's lifeless body lying on the blacktop had tears coming to her eyes and her legs feeling like they were going to give out. Before she could collapse, Hayden pulled her into his arms and held her close.

"Hey, now." His head dipped and his warm breath fell against her ear as he whispered, "He's okay. Henry's okay."

She should have pulled away, but her body refused to listen. Beneath her ear, she could hear his heart beating. It beat as rapidly as hers and she knew he had been just as scared. His concern for Henry touched her as much as the large hands that caressed her back. Her fear started to leave, replaced by a warm feeling it took her a moment to define.

She felt . . . safe.

She tried to remember the last time she had felt this way, but she couldn't pull up one memory. Not one. Even when they had been first dating, Jonathan hadn't made her feel safe. And her parents had never instilled security as much as insecurity.

But with just one hug, Hayden made her feel like nothing could harm her.

Like in the warm cocoon of his arms, she was invincible.

CHAPTER SIX

HAYDEN COULD HAVE stood there holding Paisley in his arms for the rest of his life. She fit perfectly. Like she had been specially made just for him. Her soft breasts pressed sweetly against his rib cage and her head was just the right height to rest his chin on. Her hair smelled like fresh peaches and sunshine. He took a deep breath and realized that, even after being scared out of his wits, he could still feel desire.

He just hoped Paisley couldn't feel it too.

But even if she could, he wasn't about to pull away. He was enjoying holding her too much. It was too bad Henry decided to become inquisitive.

"Hey, Hay? Why are you huggin' my mama?"

At the question, Paisley drew back and stepped away. Her cheeks were flushed and her eyes still glistened like a dew-drenched mountain meadow. It took everything in Hayden to keep from pulling her back into his arms. But the defiant set of her chin told him that their moment was over.

He looked down at Henry and answered his

question. "You scared your mama real bad, Henry James, and sometimes when people get scared, they need a hug."

Henry nodded. "Like when I had that bad nightmare about my T. rex wanting to eat me and Mama hugged me close all night."

"Sort of like that. Except nightmares aren't real. You getting hit by that truck could've happened. Especially when you do something stupid like running out in the street without looking both ways. Since you've proven you're not careful, there will be no more crossing any street without an adult. Understood?"

Henry nodded. "Yes, sir, 'cause I don't want to get a paddling. I bet you got a big paddle, Hay."

Hayden's face flushed and he shot a quick glance at Paisley before he returned his attention to Henry. "It's not my place to paddle you. I just said that because I was scared. And sometimes when you get real scared, you say things you don't mean. It doesn't make much sense, but that's how it works."

"You know what, Hay?" Henry's eyes welled with tears. "I was scared too."

Hayden's heart just about broke in two. Even though Paisley had told him to stay away from her son, he couldn't help lifting the little boy into his arms and hugging him close. "I know you were, partner. So let's never do that again."

"I won't. I prom—There's Miss Kitty!"

Hayden turned to see Kitty Carson's mail truck zipping down the street toward them. She turned in and came to a gravel-spitting stop beside them.

"Well, hey, y'all! Don't you look like the cutest little family?"

It was easy to see by the look on Paisley's face that Kitty's comment had not gone over well. She took Henry out of Hayden's arms.

"Hi, Kitty. I hope you brought the package you have for me."

"I sure did." She pulled a large envelope from the pile of mail sitting in the bag next to her. "I would've brought it sooner, but Mama's arthritis was acting up and I needed to run and get her a prescription at the pharmacy. Then I ran into Stan Tate and he got to talking—and you know how that man can talk. Before I knew it, I was running way behind getting the other mail delivered and I figured you wouldn't mind if I dropped this off a little later." She looked between Paisley and Hayden and smiled brightly. "So I guess working so closely together has made you two . . . friends."

Hayden waited to see how Paisley would answer when Henry jumped in. "Nope. Mama thinks Hay is just a saddle tramp with no dimes to rub together. But now that Hay sabed me, I bet she changed her tune." He glanced at Paisley. "Didn't you, Mama?"

Paisley's face turned bright red and Hayden felt about as low as a man could feel. Was that how she saw him? A saddle tramp who didn't have two dimes to rub together? And what did he expect? He hadn't exactly made her think otherwise. Still, it stung.

"I should get to work." He tipped his hat.

"Ladies." He winked at Henry before he headed across the street to the bar.

He felt miserable the rest of the night. Some of it had to do with Paisley thinking he was a penniless saddle tramp and some had to do with the image still stuck in his head of Henry being hit by the semitruck.

He shouldn't have threatened Henry with a spanking. It wasn't his place to discipline him. He'd just been so damn scared when he'd seen the little boy standing in the street with that eighteen-wheeler headed straight for him. The thought of what could have happened still made him feel sick.

Which meant he'd gotten too close to Henry. And if how hurt he felt over Paisley's view of him was any indication, he'd gotten too close to his mama as well. It was a relief when Everly brought in the food orders. He was terrified Paisley would read his misery and know exactly how much she had hurt him.

That night, he didn't sleep well. He tossed and turned in his bed in the bunkhouse until he finally gave up on sleeping and got up and showered before heading to the stables.

Dale White had nice stables, but they didn't compare to the Kingmans'. The outside of the massive building that housed all the Kingmans' thoroughbreds was made of Austin stone and natural wood with a state-of-the-art steel door that easily slid open when Hayden punched in the code. The inside had a high-beamed ceiling and a brick-paved aisle that led to all the stalls.

From the moment Hayden had first seen the stables, he'd felt like he'd stepped into heaven. He had spent a lot of his twenties working cattle when bronc riding hadn't paid the bills. But horses were his first love. Just the smell of hay and horse manure soothed his depression and, as soon as the Kingmans' thoroughbred colt popped his head over the door of his stall, Hayden couldn't help smiling.

"Good mornin', Glory Boy." Hayden walked over and greeted the colt with a pat on his withers. "It looks like you're up early too." The colt bobbed his head in agreement and Hayden laughed as he stroked the horse's well-groomed coat. Everyone on the ranch loved Glory Boy and showered him with attention. Including Hayden. "So what's your problem? You're too young for girl troubles. But you just wait. It's coming. And believe me, there's nothing harder. Especially when you fall for a woman you have no business falling for."

Hayden knew some folks would think he was crazy standing there talking to a horse about his problems, but he'd discovered long ago that talking to animals always helped him figure things out.

"She's been hurt, Glory. She's been hurt real bad by her ex-husband—or hell, maybe she isn't even divorced yet. Which makes me more pathetic falling for a married woman. And even if she was single, she wouldn't want to get wrapped up with a saddle tramp loser like me. She's used to a much better lifestyle than I can give her.

Everly said Paisley and Henry lived in the biggest house in town and she drives a Range Rover that probably cost ten times more than my old pickup. She's smart and college educated while I'm just an ex-rodeo bum who barely made it through high school. She deserves better than what I can offer her."

"Funny thing about women. The good ones don't care about college diplomas and money as much as love."

Hayden startled and turned to see Uncle Jack standing in the open door of the stables.

Jack Kingman had been the previous owner of Nasty Jack's bar. He was the brother of Charlie "King" Kingman and the Kingman siblings' great-uncle. He lived at the Kingman Ranch, and at eighty-three, spent his days napping or playing cards or dominos with the family cook, Potts, or chess with the stable manager, Tab. Occasionally, he would show up at the bar and sit at a back table drinking whiskey. Hayden had tried starting up a conversation with the man, but Uncle Jack wasn't much of a talker. He seemed to be more of a watcher. Hayden had caught him watching him more times than he could count.

Just like he was doing now.

"Good mornin', Mr. Kingman," Hayden said.

"Like I told you before, Uncle Jack will do."

Hayden nodded, but there was no way he'd feel comfortable calling the man uncle. "So is there something you needed, sir?"

His eyes squinted. "If I tell you, are you going to tell my overprotective nieces and nephews?"

"I guess that depends on what it is?"

Uncle Jack snorted. "Then I guess it's my secret to keep. Although I seem to have overheard your secret." He arched a bushy white eyebrow. "So you're in love with a married woman."

Hayden wanted to deny it. But since Uncle Jack had already overheard him spilling his guts, it was pointless. "It seems that way."

Uncle Jack shuffled over. "And she doesn't love you?"

He sighed. "No, sir. I'm not even sure she likes me."

"Is she still in love with her husband?"

Hayden realized he couldn't answer the question. He would hope Paisley wasn't still in love with a man who had abused her, but he didn't know for sure. "I don't know."

Uncle Jack shook his head. "Then you are in a pickle. But that's love for you. It would be much easier if it made sense. If the people you fall for also fell for you. But after sixty years of running a bar and listening to every sob story to come down the pike, I've discovered love doesn't make a bit of sense. It just shows up on your doorstep one day and you have to deal with it."

Hayden sat down on a bale of hay and ran a hand over his face. "I wish I had just ignored it like my mama ignores the Jehovah's Witnesses when they ring the doorbell."

Uncle Jack snorted. "If we could do that, life would be a lot easier. Of course, it wouldn't be nearly as much fun." He sat down on an opposite bale of hay. "You don't think you have a chance with this woman?"

"Slim at best."

"Slim is better than no chance at all."

Uncle Jack did have a point. There had been a brief moment while Hayden had held Paisley when he'd felt her release the tight rein she kept on her emotions and melt into his body. Was it possible she had felt even a glimmer of attraction toward him?

He shook his head. "I'm a hopeless fool."

"We all are from time to time." Uncle Jack glanced at the stalls of horses and a sad look entered his eyes. "Especially when we get old. Our brain tells us we can do things our bodies can no longer do."

Hayden suddenly realized why Uncle Jack was there. "You came out here to go riding?"

Uncle Jack shrugged. "See, a hopeless fool. I keep dreaming about riding a horse again when I can't even lift a damn saddle. But that doesn't stop me from coming out here every so often to try."

An eighty-three-year-old man had no business being on a horse. If one of the Kingmans found out Hayden had helped him and Uncle Jack got hurt, there would be hell to pay. But Hayden understood the old guy's problem. Hayden had kept bronc riding long after his body and doctors had told him to stop. Sometimes you just had to figure things out on your own.

"I'll saddle a horse for you."

Uncle Jack stared at him. "Without telling anyone?"

"Not a soul."

Hayden chose the sweetest-tempered mare to saddle. He led the horse out to the paddock. It was still dark, but as soon as Hayden stepped out, the motion-sensor light lit up the paddock. He tied the horse's reins to the railing and then placed the steps Stetson had made for his wife Lily next to the horse. Surprisingly, Uncle Jack had no problems getting up the steps or into the saddle. The expression of pure joy on his face eased some of Hayden's concerns about whether or not this was a good idea. Now he just prayed the old guy could stay in the saddle.

Uncle Jack did.

In fact, it was obvious by the way he handled the horse that he knew what he was doing. Still, Hayden got a little nervous when, after he walked the horse around the paddock a few times, he urged him into a trot. Thankfully, he only lasted a couple go-arounds before he reined the horse in.

"That will about do it for this old body."

Once Hayden helped Uncle Jack down, he walked the horse back into the stables to unsaddle him. When he came out of the stall, he found Uncle Jack sitting on a bale of hay looking a little worse for wear. "You okay?"

Uncle Jack flashed him a smile. "It was much easier in my dreams."

Hayden laughed. "I bet it was. And maybe that's where it needs to stay."

Uncle Jack got up and winced. "You might have a good point. You hungry? 'Cause I'm suddenly starving. Come on up to the house. Everyone is probably still sleeping, but I'm sure Potts will have something ready to eat."

Hayden hesitated. "That's okay. I'll just grab something in the bunkhouse."

Uncle Jack stared him down. "I'm not asking you to come back to the house to be nice. I'm asking you because I need help. My ass feels like it's been peppered with buckshot."

Since Hayden was responsible for Uncle Jack's sore butt, he had no choice but to help the old guy back to the house. He intended to leave him at the back door and make his excuses, but Uncle Jack knew exactly what to say to get him to accept.

"You scared to come in, boy? Do my nephews and nieces intimidate you?"

With a grumbled, "Not hardly," Hayden followed Uncle Jack into the house.

While he had been in every stable, barn, and warehouse on the ranch, he had never been inside Buckinghorse Palace. The Kingmans had invited him to meals before, but he'd always found an excuse to decline. He didn't belong in a fancy castle.

Except inside it didn't look like a fancy castle. The mudroom looked like any other ranch mudroom. There was a row of sweat-stained cowboy hats hanging on hooks along one wall. On the other wall were winter dusters and rain slickers. Muddy boots were lined up beneath a bench. Hayden sat down on the bench and started to take off his boots, but Uncle Jack stopped him.

"Unless you have shit or mud on them, boots are allowed in the house."

Hayden checked to make sure his boots were clean before he followed Uncle Jack into the kitchen. The kitchen *was* big and fancy with nice stainless-steel appliances and granite countertops, but it still had a comfortable, homey feel. The long harvest table was scarred and the numerous chairs surrounding it mismatched and well worn. The old cook stood at the stove cooking something that made Hayden's stomach growl.

"What's for breakfast, Potts?" Uncle Jack asked.

Potts startled and turned, wielding a wooden spoon like a weapon. He relaxed when he saw them. "What has you two up so early?"

"I wanted to get in a little riding this morning," Uncle Jack said with a wink to Hayden.

Potts laughed as he went back to his cooking. "Sure you did, you old goat. Mornin', Hayden. You stayin' for breakfast?"

"He sure is," Uncle Jack answered for him as he took a seat at the table. When Hayden didn't sit down right away, Uncle Jack glared at him. "Well, sit down, boy. You want me to get a crick in my neck to go with the pain in my ass?"

Breakfast turned out to be cheesy eggs, maple bacon, and a casserole that tasted like cinnamon French toast. The entire time Hayden filled his stomach with the delicious meal, Potts and Uncle Jack bickered like two old biddies about everything from horses to what was the best pie Gretchen made. Not wanting to be there when the rest of the family got up, Hayden quickly ate, and then took his plate and coffee cup to the sink.

Uncle Jack was standing there when he turned. "I'll show you around the house before you go. I'm sure, like everyone else, you're curious about this ridiculous monstrosity my brother built."

Hayden started to say there was no need, but there was a need. It was the same need that had brought him to the Kingman Ranch. Curiosity mixed with a good dose of stupidity.

Uncle Jack started with a tour of the main floor. He showed him Stetson's impressive study and a huge dining room that could easily seat forty people before leading him into a room with a massive stone fireplace and leather furniture that probably cost more than Hayden had in his savings account. He'd been so proud of his nest egg—and the small chunk of land he'd purchased for his own horse ranch—but the expensive furnishings made him feel like he didn't have more than two dimes to rub together.

Above the fireplace was a portrait. Hayden couldn't stop himself from walking over and taking a closer look.

"That's my brother, Charlie," Uncle Jack said. "Or King, as he liked to be called."

King was a big man. He covered the entire canvas with his broad shoulders and barrel chest. The eyes peering out from beneath the brown cowboy hat were dark and intense. There was a stern set to his mouth.

"He looks like Stetson," Hayden said. "Or Stetson looks like him."

"Stetson is a lot like King, but Stet has a softer side. King was a hard man."

From what Hayden had pieced together from talking to the family and ranch hands, King had swindled Uncle Jack out of his share of the ranch. Something Jack had not forgiven the family for easily. It had been Wolfe who brought an end to the feud, but only after Jack's grandson had tried to get revenge on the Kingmans and had died in the fire he'd set.

"I heard you didn't get along with your brother," Hayden said as he continued to look at the portrait.

Uncle Jack sighed behind him. "Family can get complicated. Both Charlie and I were too stubborn and unbending. I wanted to blame him for taking away my share of the ranch. But the truth is that it was my own fault. I let my own insecurities keep me from claiming what was rightfully mine."

Hayden turned around. "It looks like you're back where you belong now."

Uncle Jack studied him. "Looks like you are too."

Hayden laughed uneasily. "I don't belong here. My home is in Montana."

"I heard that was your birthplace. But homes aren't where you're born. They're the place you choose to live." He paused. "Like your mama. She might have been born in Houston, but she chose Montana as her home."

Everything inside of Hayden froze and all he could do was stare at Uncle Jack as he continued.

"It took me a while to figure it out. Thirty-three years is a long time. But my long-term memory is much better than my short-term. Your mama worked as a maid right here on this very ranch that summer. I remember her because she came into Nasty Jack's almost every night. Not to drink, but to dance. At first, she had a lot of partners. By the end of the summer, she only had one." Uncle Jack paused. "You have her eyes. But everything else is pure Kingman."

CHAPTER SEVEN

PAISLEY WAS RUNNING . . . or trying to. The faster she attempted to move her feet, the slower they went. Behind her, she could hear the click of snake-leather cowboy boots coming up the stairs of Hester's house.

Jonathan was getting closer.

She could hear him repeating the same words over and over again in a low, threatening voice. "Over your dead body."

She tried to yell a warning to Henry to run and hide. But she couldn't get a sound to come out of her mouth. When she reached the end of the hallway where his room was located, there was nothing but a ledge that dropped down into nothingness.

The click of boots grew louder.

She turned and saw Jonathan moving toward her down the dark hallway. The look on his face was the same look he always got when he was about to hit her: a mixture of rage and glee. He raised his hand. But instead of hitting her, Henry dangled from his fist.

"Help me, Mama!" Henry screamed. "Help me!"

She made a lunge for her son. Before she could reach him, Jonathan released his grip and Henry dropped over the ledge into the darkness beyond. Paisley was able to scream then. She screamed in one long, pain-filled scream as she dove off the ledge after her son.

With her heart racing, Paisley startled awake. She lay there for a moment trying to recover from the nightmare. She sat up and glanced around the room. Dawn peeked in through the crack in the curtains, tinting the entire room in a purple haze.

Jumping out of bed, she hurried to the room next door. She stopped in the doorway and heaved a sigh of relief when she saw Henry sleeping peacefully amid a tangle of blankets and stuffed animals. As he'd done ever since he was a baby, he'd kicked off the covers and his pajama-covered butt stuck up in the air. Paisley walked over and sat down on the edge of the bed, placing a shaky hand on his back. As she felt the rhythmic rise and fall of his lungs expanding, her tension eased and she said a prayer of thanks that it had only been a dream.

Although the nightmare wasn't over.

Over Your Dead Body.

The words had been embossed on Paisley's brain ever since she had pulled the divorce papers out of the envelope and seen the words scrawled across the front page of the documents in black Sharpie.

Deep down, she had known Jonathan wouldn't

make things easy. But she hadn't thought he would so openly threaten her. He usually kept his rage well hidden. Especially from his father, a man Jonathan feared and revered. It had taken Paisley threatening to show his father the pictures she'd taken of her face after he had beaten her for Jonathan to agree to the divorce in the first place.

Now, it looked like he'd changed his mind . . . and gone off the deep end. She had felt his rage in every letter slashed across the paper.

After opening the envelope, Paisley had immediately called her lawyer and texted a photo of the threat. Her lawyer had calmed her and told her that it wasn't unusual for people to get upset and say things they didn't mean while going through a divorce. They would just file for a default divorce where they wouldn't need his signature. There was nothing to worry about.

But her lawyer didn't know Jonathan. He wasn't the type of person to give empty threats. If he said it, he meant it. Paisley had spent the last two days in a state of constant stress and nerves. She had wanted to tell Everly, but she knew her sister would go ballistic and want to head to Mesaville and confront Jonathan.

Although Everly probably knew something was wrong. The last two nights at the bar, Paisley had dropped and broken numerous glasses and messed up more than a few food orders.

Not that she had delivered those orders to Hayden.

She had been avoiding him again. Partly because she was embarrassed over what Henry had told him about her thinking he was a good-for-nothing saddle tramp. And partly because of the feelings he'd ignited when he'd held her in his arms.

Just like Henry felt when Hayden had swept him out of danger's way, being in Hayden's arms had made Paisley feel saved.

"Everything okay?"

The softly spoken words startled Paisley out of her thoughts. She turned to see Hester standing in the doorway. She was a spooky sight in her full-length black robe with her long silver hair swirling wildly around her face and shoulders. The purplish light of dawn made her eyes look even more violet and intense.

Paisley got up from the bed. "I was just checking on Henry."

Hester nodded as she stepped back into the hallway so Paisley could exit the room. "I used to do the same thing with Aurora and Mystic when they were little."

Aurora was Hester's daughter and Mystic's mother. From what Paisley had pieced together, Aurora was a psychic like her mother, but also a wanderer who didn't stay in one place for very long. She had dropped Mystic off with Hester when Mystic was only a toddler and Hester had raised her granddaughter. Paisley couldn't understand how a parent could desert their child.

She glanced back at Henry. She couldn't live if anything happened to him. The scare she'd had the other day reinforced her belief.

Now another truck was headed straight for him.

If Jonathan had so easily gotten into Hester's house before, he could do it again. Next time, Henry might be here. And Hester. Neither one of them would stand by and let Jonathan hurt her. She couldn't stomach the thought of Jonathan turning his rage on them.

Which left only one thing to do.

"I've been thinking it's time I found another place to live," she blurted out. She expected Hester to try and talk her out of it and was surprised when she didn't.

"I agree." Hester closed the door to Henry's room. "I don't think it's safe here."

Paisley's heart started to race again. "Did you see something?"

Hester touched the amethyst that always hung from a chain around her neck and closed her eyes. "I see a darkness. The same darkness I saw before."

"Does it touch Henry? Is Henry hurt?"

Hester shook her head. "No. A queen will save him. A powerful queen will vanquish the darkness before it can harm him." She opened her eyes and smiled. "With the help of a king. A king in disguise."

Paisley wished she could take Hester's prediction to heart. But a powerful queen? A king in disguise? It sounded too much like the television series *Game of Thrones* that Hester loved to watch, to be anything more than her trying to ease Paisley's mind. But Hester had one thing right. Paisley did need to leave here and find a safe place for her and Henry to stay. A place where Jonathan couldn't easily get to them.

But where?

They could move in with Everly and Chance. She knew her sister would welcome them with open arms. Everly had been trying to get them to move in with her since she'd married Chance. But Paisley didn't want to impose on newlyweds. And the parsonage would be the first place Jonathan would look if they weren't at Hester's. While Chance had no problem dealing with Jonathan before, she didn't want to put him in that position again. He was pastor of a large congregation. He didn't have time to be her and Henry's bodyguard.

Hester's hand touched her arm, bringing her out of her thoughts. "It will all work out. Why don't you go and get showered and dressed. Then we'll worry about what needs to be done."

"Thank you, Hester, but you don't need to concern yourself with my problems."

Hester smiled. "Problems are solved much easier when they're shared."

Paisley didn't realize how much sharing Hester planned on doing until she came down the stairs no more than an hour later and stepped into the kitchen. Everly, Chance, Shane, and Delaney were all sitting at the breakfast nook table. Everly didn't beat around the bush on why they were there.

"What's going on, Paise? And don't tell me nothing. You've been a nervous wreck for the last two days. And now Hester calls us and says we need to find you a safe place to stay. Did Jonathan show up again? Because if he did—"

"No." Paisley cut her off. "He didn't show up." She hesitated before telling the truth. "He just . . . wrote something on the divorce papers."

"What?"

"Over your dead body."

Everly jumped up. "That sonofabitch! I'll show him whose body is going to be dead."

Chance reached out and pulled Everly into his lap. "Calm down, Ev. You losing your temper isn't going to help your sister. Hester is right. We need to come up with a safe place for Paisley and Henry to stay. And I think Shane and Delaney have the right idea. Paisley and Henry will be safest at the Kingman Ranch."

Paisley shook her head. "Absolutely not. I'm not going to impose on the Kingmans."

"It's not an imposition," Delaney said. "We have plenty of room." She placed a hand on her rounded stomach and smiled. "Although we are filling those rooms pretty darn quickly. If these two act anything like Buck and I, they're going to need separate bedrooms or they'll end up killing each other."

Everly turned to Delaney and Shane with shock. "Two? You're having twins?"

Shane beamed proudly as he hooked an arm around his wife's shoulders. "We just found out yesterday at Del's ultrasound. One little tyke is for sure a boy, but the other one stubbornly refused to give us a clear view." He winked at Delaney.

"Which leads me to believe that it's a feisty girl just like her mama." He looked at Hester. "Any insights, Hessy?"

Hester smiled knowingly. "None that I'm willing to share. I think it will be nice if you two have a surprise." She glanced at Everly. "In fact, I think there are going to be a lot of surprises this year."

Everly's eyes widened. "I'm not pregnant."

Hester's smile got bigger. "Yet."

Chance laughed as he hugged his wife close. "I guess we need to get busy, honey. We don't want to ruin Hester's prediction percentage . . . or let my brother win by two."

Everly shot him a look over her shoulder. "Get busy? If we get any busier in the bedroom, Preach, we'll be too exhausted to do anything else."

Chance blushed. "Point taken. And at the moment, we have other concerns." He looked at Paisley. "Like keeping you and Henry safe. The ranch is the safest place, Paise. There is no way Jonathan can show up there and not be seen by a dozen cowboys who will be happy to show him the way out."

"Or cowgirls." Delaney's eyes glittered with anger. "I would love to get a piece of a man who has nothing better to do than threaten the mother of his child."

"Thank you for the offer," Paisley said. "But it's my problem. Not y'all's. And certainly not the entire ranch's. I don't want anyone to get hurt because of me."

"You need to stop that, Paisley," Everly scolded. "You aren't responsible for what Jonathan does.

You and Henry are moving to the Kingman Ranch and that's final."

Before Paisley could continue to argue, Henry appeared in the doorway of the kitchen in his dinosaur pajamas with his hair sticking up. His eyes were wide and she knew what was going to come out of his mouth as soon as he opened it.

"I want to mobe to the Kingman Ranch! I want to mobe to the Kingman Ranch!"

Before Paisley could explain to him that they weren't moving to the Kingman Ranch, Everly chimed in. "Well, of course you do. Who wouldn't want to live on a ranch with a bunch of cool cowboys who I'm sure will be happy to teach you how to ride a horse and lasso a steer?"

That was all it took for Henry to go ballistic and start jumping around and squealing at the top of his lungs about riding horses and lassoing cows. By the smirk on Everly's face, she knew exactly what she'd done.

Still, Paisley might have kept on refusing if Hester hadn't spoken. "I know you don't want to be a burden to anyone, Paisley. But sometimes you have to take the help that's offered you. Not just for yourself, but for your son."

Hester was right. This wasn't about Paisley. It was about Henry. She had to keep her son safe. No matter how much she hated imposing on people she barely knew . . . or how much she didn't want to be living on the same ranch as Hayden West.

If she were honest, Hayden was the main reason she didn't want to move to the ranch. The way he made her feel scared her. She had thought she'd never want to be with another man again, and yet, she'd so easily fallen into Hayden's arms . . . and wanted to stay there. She'd fallen into Jonathan's arms just as easily.

Jonathan had convinced her that he was the type of man she could trust. The type of man who would take her away from the fake reality her parents had wanted her to live in and give her an authentic life. A life where she could feel loved for who she was.

How wrong she had been. Instead of moving to a safe, loving environment where she could be herself, she had just exchanged prison guards. She wasn't about to put her faith in another man. If she wanted her son to feel safe and loved, it was up to her.

Right now, the Kingman Ranch *was* the best option for protecting her son. And it wasn't like she would be living in the same house with Hayden. He stayed in the bunkhouse with the other ranch hands and she and Henry would be staying at Buckinghorse Palace. It would be easy to avoid him.

"Fine," she said. "I'll move to the Kingman Ranch, but just until the divorce is final." She looked at Everly. "And I'm still going to help you out at the bar."

"No, you're not. I can't bartend and worry about you. Jonathan could come into the bar when it's crowded and no one would be the wiser. Chance said he'll help me out for the next couple weeks."

Everly sent her husband an evil smile. "Believe me, I'll love ordering him around."

Chance winked. "I think I've proven I can take orders."

"Then it's settled," Hester said. "Paisley and Henry will move to the Kingman Ranch."

Henry's squeals could be heard in the next county. "I'm gonna be a cowboy! I'm gonna be a cowboy!"

CHAPTER EIGHT

"WHAT THE HELL do you mean you're leaving?" Stetson stared at Hayden in disbelief. "Why?"

There were a lot of reasons Hayden had decided to leave the Kingman Ranch: He owned a chunk of land in Montana just waiting for him to start his dream ranch. He missed his mama and stepdaddy. The woman he'd fallen in love with thought he was nothing but a no-account saddle tramp.

And his secret was out.

While Uncle Jack had said Douglas Kingman being Hayden's father was Hayden's secret to share, Hayden knew it was only a matter of time before his half siblings figured it out. He didn't want that to happen. The Kingmans had endured enough hell with their father's infidelity. They didn't need living proof of it. Nor did Hayden want them thinking he'd come there to get money or a piece of their ranch. It would be better for everyone if he left well enough alone and just disappeared from the Kingmans' lives.

Uncle Jack didn't agree. The old guy thought

Hayden should tell the truth and claim his place in the Kingman family.

But he was wrong.

This wasn't his home. This wasn't his family. His home and family were in Montana. He needed to get back there.

Unfortunately, Stetson seemed to be as adamant about Hayden staying as Uncle Jack was.

"If you leaving has to do with a raise, I was just about to offer you one. In fact, I'm offering you the position of horse breeding manager. You've proven you know horses better than anyone on this ranch—although don't tell Delaney I said that or I'll never hear the end of it. With the new position, you'll get a healthy raise and a room in the house right off the kitchen. Don't tell me you wouldn't love getting out of the bunkhouse and having your own private bathroom."

Hayden shook his head. "Nope, I can't tell you that having a bathroom to myself wouldn't be nice. But my leaving isn't about living in the bunkhouse. Nor does it have to do with a raise or a promotion. I never planned on staying in Texas, Stetson. My home is Montana."

Stetson sat back in his leather desk chair with a huff. "Montana? All they have in Montana is a bunch of trees that cattle can get lost in. There's no better place to be a cowboy than right here in Texas where you can see as far as the eye. And if this is about not wanting to leave your mama and daddy, I'm sure we can find them a nice little house in Cursed. You said your daddy was a carpenter, right? We can always use a good carpenter around the ranch. And your mama could help out at the house. Or in the garden if she likes flowers and plants."

Hayden wasn't about to ask his parents to move to the Kingman Ranch. Not only because of what happened to his mama when she worked there, but also because he hadn't been truthful with them. They thought he was working on a ranch in Wyoming. While he was sure his mother would understand his need to meet his half siblings, he wasn't so sure his stepfather would. Jimmy was his father in all the ways that counted. He had raised Hayden like his own and Hayden worried he'd be hurt if he found out he'd come to Texas looking for more information about his biological father.

"That's real nice of you, but my parents are quite happy in Montana," Hayden said. "And I bought a little piece of land there that I plan to turn into my own horse ranch."

The stubborn set of Stetson's jaw relaxed and he released a long sigh. "Well, I can't argue with a man wanting to run his own ranch. But I hope you'll at least give me two weeks' notice to find someone else." He paused. "Not that I'll be able to replace you."

Before Hayden could get over his surprise at Stetson's compliment, Lily peeked her head in.

Lily was a petite, dark-haired woman with the kind of soft, soothing voice that made a person want to listen to her talk all day. She smiled at Hayden before turning that smile on her husband. Stetson looked like his teen crush had just walked into the room. Worshipful was too mild a word to describe the look on his face.

"Hey, baby," he said.

Lily's smile got even brighter. "Hey, yourself. I'm sorry to interrupt, but our new guests are here and I'd thought you'd want to greet them."

"Thanks, honey," Stetson said. "I'll be right there."

When the door closed, Hayden couldn't help asking, "Guests?"

Stetson got up and moved around the desk. "Everly's sister and nephew are coming to stay with us for the next couple weeks."

Hayden's entire body tensed as he stood. "Why? I thought they were staying with Hester Malone."

"They were, but I guess Paisley's soon-to-be ex-husband threatened her and everyone agrees she and her son will be safer here."

Hayden didn't realize he had clenched his hands into fists until Stetson spoke.

"If you want to punch something, I'd recommend the punching bag out in the bunkhouse. Adeline just had this room painted and refurnished."

Hayden released his fists and took a deep breath. "Sorry, it just pisses me off that a man would force a woman and her child into hiding. I regret not beating the sonofabitch to a pulp when I had the chance. Paisley has been through enough and now this."

Stetson studied him. "So I guess you've gotten close to Paisley since working at the bar."

"Close? No. I wouldn't say we're close. I just hate bullies."

As soon as Hayden and Stetson stepped out of the study, Henry came racing up and launched himself at Hayden.

"Hay!"

Hayden caught him and hugged him close before setting him back on his feet. "Hey, partner."

Henry beamed up at him from beneath the brim of his hat. "Guess what, Hay? I'm going to libe here. Right here in Buckinghorse Castle. Just like a real cowboy. And Aunt Eberly says you'll teach me how to ride horses and rope steers and scoop horse poop."

"Your aunt did not say that."

Hayden's heart picked up its pace at the sound of Paisley's voice. His gaze snapped over to see her standing in the foyer with Lily, Adeline, and Gretchen. The other women were beautiful, but only Paisley took his breath away. She wore jeans that molded to her long legs and a soft yellow sweater that molded to her full breasts. Her hair fell in soft curls around her face and shoulders, blending with the sweater and making her shine brighter than the sunlight beaming down from the skylight.

There he stood in a sweaty flannel shirt and dirty jeans looking like a no-account saddle tramp.

He pulled off his hat and nodded. "Paisley."

Her cheeks flushed a rosy pink that only made her look even more breathtaking. "Hay."

The way his name came out of her lips made him feel all lightheaded and loopy. They stood there staring at each other for what felt like forever before Stetson cleared his throat and spoke.

"Welcome to Kingman Ranch, Paisley."

When Paisley turned her attention to Stetson, Hayden tapped the brim of Henry's hat and winked at him. "I'll catch you later, partner."

Once outside, Hayden released his breath in a long sigh and tried to get a handle on his emotions. Damn, he couldn't even be in the same room with the woman without acting like a lovesick idiot. Her being here was just another reason to leave.

But first he had to know what Jonathan had done to her.

He pulled his cellphone out of his pocket and called Everly. She answered on the first ring.

"What's up, hot cowboy?"

"How did Jonathan threaten your sister?"

"So I guess Paisley got to the ranch okay. I wanted to drive her and Henry, but she left before I got up this morning. Stubborn woman."

"It seems to run in your family. So what did Jonathan do?"

"He wrote *Over your dead body* on the divorce papers." Her voice trembled with anger. "I can't tell you how much I want to go to Mesaville and beat his ass."

Hayden couldn't agree more, but he wasn't about to let Everly know. She'd be there to pick him up in two seconds flat. And if Hayden went to Mesaville, he was going alone.

"Chance is convinced it's just an empty threat," Everly continued. "Empty threat or not, it's rattled Paisley. She's been a nervous wreck the past few days. But now that she's at the ranch, I'm sure she'll calm down. I know I feel much better with her being there. Not just because all the Kingmans and Shane will be watching out for her and Henry, but also because you will." She hesitated. "I might not be the type to give people a lot of praise, but you're a good man, Hayden. I knew that the first time I met you. I trust you and know you'll do everything you can to protect my sister and nephew."

There went Hayden's plans to leave. It wasn't just because Everly trusted him. If he left the ranch and something happened to Paisley and Henry, he'd never forgive himself.

"I'll watch over them," he vowed. "But I need a promise from you. If Jonathan shows up, you need to call the sheriff immediately, Everly. Don't take matters into your own hands. I mean it."

There was a long hesitation before she sighed. "Fine. But if you get your hands on him, kick his ass for me."

That was a promise he had no problem making.

After getting off the phone with Everly, he texted Stetson.

I'll stay a few more weeks and I'll take you up on that offer of a room.

If he was going to keep an eye on Paisley and Henry, he needed to be closer than the bunkhouse.

Hayden spent the rest of the morning working in the stables. He was grooming Glory Boy when he heard a commotion outside. He walked out to see three ranch hands fighting to control a horse that had just been taken out of a trailer. It was Dale White's high-strung stallion, Royal Duke. Stetson had told him that he was going to try to buy the stud. Hayden should have known his stubborn half brother would succeed.

Although it didn't look like he'd made a good deal.

High strung wasn't the best way to describe the horse. Royal Duke was a hellion. The dents in the side of the trailer he'd been transported in were proof. As was the hell he was giving the ranch hands.

"Open the paddock gate," Hayden yelled as he took the reins from the ranch hand who was struggling to keep the horse from rearing. Hayden didn't try to restrain the animal. He loosened the reins and let him fight. When the horse pulled one way, Hayden moved with him, slowly guiding him toward the paddock. Once they were inside and the gate was closed, Hayden released the reins. The horse took off, racing first one way around the fence line and then the other. It didn't take long for the stallion to tire out and come to a dead stop, huffing loudly as he glared at Hayden.

"Hey, boy," Hayden said in a soft voice. "Remember me. You're looking a lot more peppy today."

The horse snorted and shook his head as Hayden moved closer.

"Yeah, I guess it wasn't fun to ride in a bumpy

trailer and come to a new place where you don't know anyone. But this here is the Kingman Ranch. It's about the best horse ranch in Texas . . . maybe the world. So you should consider yourself lucky. You're gonna like it here. It's okay if you're a little spunky. All the Kingmans are a little spunky too."

"What's spunky, Hay?"

Hayden turned to find Henry standing on the fence railing next to the gate. Stetson stood directly behind him with his hands braced on either side so Henry wouldn't fall. Paisley stood next to Stetson with her green eyes pinned on Hayden. It took a real effort to pull his gaze away and open the paddock gate. Once the gate was closed behind him, he answered Henry's question.

"Spunky is what you are sometimes when you're racing around and getting wild."

Henry grinned. "I like being spunky."

Hayden and Stetson laughed. Paisley didn't. Hayden figured to a mama spunky wasn't all that funny.

"It is fun to race around and get wild," he said. "But there are times to be spunky and there are times to settle down and do what you're supposed to do. You need to learn that and so does Royal Duke."

"Royal Duke? Is that his name?"

"It is," Stetson said. "What do you think?"

Henry scrunched his face. "I don't like it."

"Henry," Paisley scolded. "Don't be rude."

Stetson lifted Henry off the fence and set

him on the ground. "I don't care for the name either. So what do you think we should call him, Henry?"

Henry squinted his eyes in thought a moment before he grinned. "Spunky."

Stetson laughed. "Then Spunky it is."

Henry turned to Hayden. "Can I ride him, Hay? Can I?"

Before Hayden could say no, Paisley cut in. "Absolutely not. Like I said before, you're too young to start riding."

By the look on Henry's face, it wasn't hard to figure out that a tantrum was coming. Before it could, Hayden placed a hand on his shoulder and redirected his attention.

"Have you ever seen a colt, partner?"

Henry shook his head. "What's a colt?"

"It's a male horse under the age of five."

"I'm fibe."

"I know. That's why I thought you'd like to meet Glory Boy."

"Glory Boy. I like that name. Can I meet him now?"

"You need to ask your mama first. And if she says no, you can't get spunky or I won't issue the invitation again."

Henry looked at his mother. "Can I, Mama? Can I go see Glory Boy?"

Paisley hesitated for only a moment before she nodded. "Okay, but not for long. I'm sure Hayden has other jobs he needs to do."

Hayden did have plenty of jobs to do and the

biggest one stared back at him with pretty green eyes that made him melt.

As soon as Henry saw Glory Boy, he was smitten. The colt seemed to feel the same way. Hayden had never seen a horse attach itself to a human so quickly. Within minutes, Glory Boy was nuzzling Henry and making him giggle. Paisley, who stood at the stall door with Stetson, had a warm smile on her face as she watched her son and the colt. Not wanting to push his luck, Hayden brought an end to the meeting.

"It's about time to let Glory out for some exercise and you probably need to get back to the house for lunch."

Henry looked thoroughly disappointed. Paisley surprised Hayden when she spoke. "You can come see him again after lunch." She shot a glance at Hayden. "If it's okay with Hayden."

It was more than okay with Hayden. The closer Paisley and Henry were, the easier it would be to keep an eye on them. "I'll see you after lunch, partner."

Henry began to chatter excitedly about getting to see Glory Boy again as his mother took his hand and led him out of the stables. Try as he might, Hayden couldn't keep his gaze from wandering down to the curves of Paisley's butt in the snug-fitting jeans. When she and Henry disappeared around the corner of the stable door, he turned to find Stetson standing there with a smirk on his face.

"So that's what changed your mind about leaving in such an all-fire hurry."

"It's not what you think. I'm just worried about her and Henry and don't want to leave until I'm sure they're okay."

Stetson's smirk grew bigger. "And that was a real worried look you had on your face when you were staring at her butt."

Hayden scowled. "Okay. So I'm attracted to her. But it doesn't make any difference. Paisley's not interested. She's been through too much."

Stetson nodded. "She has been through a lot. But I still think she's interested. She has as much trouble keeping her eyes off you as you do keeping yours off her." He grinned. "Which leads me to believe all you need is time to tame the skittish filly like you tamed Spunky."

CHAPTER NINE

PAISLEY HAD WORRIED she'd feel like a guest at the Kingman Ranch who everyone felt like they had to put on airs for. But her fears were groundless.

The Kingmans didn't put on airs.

They were welcoming and kind to Paisley and Henry, but not one person changed their behavior because they had guests.

Lunch was complete chaos. Buck and Delaney got in a fight over the last grilled cheese sandwich and Potts had to smack their hands with his wooden spoon to get them to stop. Uncle Jack fell asleep and snored so loudly that it gave Henry the giggles. As did Danny throwing his teething biscuit and hitting Wolfe in the eye. Lily got after Stetson for giving Teddy a taste of the brownie frosting. Teddy screamed so loudly when he didn't get more that it started the other babies screaming. Gretchen and Wolfe got in an argument about her going back to work at Nasty Jack's. The argument ended when Maribelle had a major diaper explosion. Which had Henry laughing even harder and Delaney looking at Shane with a scared expression and saying, "Please tell me that's not what I'm in for."

While Henry seemed to be thoroughly entertained, Paisley felt more than a little stunned. Mealtime at the Kingmans' was the complete opposite of what she was used to. Growing up, Everly and Paisley had been expected to keep quiet at the dinner table while their parents made stilted conversation. Meals at Jonathan's family home were just as painful. His father presided over the table like he presided over a courtroom. No one talked unless the judge spoke to them first. Henry had been completely ignored.

He wasn't ignored at the Kingman table. Wolfe and Gage taught him how to dip his grilled cheese into his tomato soup and Buck told him knock-knock jokes and Delaney told him humorous stories about her pygmy goats that she'd named after the seven dwarfs. Adeline wiped his shirt off when he dribbled soup on it and Lily cut him an extra piece of brownie and Gretchen asked him what his favorite pie was and promised to make it for him. Shane offered to take him down to the refuge barn as soon as lunch was over. The only Kingman not at the table was Mystic. She was working at her salon, but Buck said she'd be there for dinner.

Paisley figured dinner would be just like lunch. Loud, chaotic . . . and overflowing with love.

Her parents had taught her love was quiet and reserved. They taught her if you loved someone, you kept your mouth shut and gave up your own wants and desires for theirs.

But here was a family who loved in a different way. No one seemed to be sacrificing their own personalities to make others happy. Everyone had no problem voicing their thoughts and opinions. Amid all the chaos, love flourished like it had never flourished in Paisley's childhood home. Or her married one.

"I guess this isn't quite what you're used to."

Adeline's words pulled Paisley from her thoughts and she tried to act like she hadn't been sitting there in stunned shock.

"Oh, no," she said. "It's . . . lovely."

Adeline laughed. "I don't think that word has ever been used to describe Kingman family meals."

"To me it *is* lovely. I like that your family doesn't mince words. My parents didn't believe in giving their children the freedom to express themselves. Which explains why I struggle expressing my true feelings."

"Believe me, I understand. I used to keep my true feelings hidden too." Adeline glanced at Stetson who was cradling Teddy in his arms and smiled. "Stetson not only had the responsibility of the ranch after our father died, but he also had the responsibility of our family. While Wolfe, Delaney, and Buck constantly went up against him, I didn't want to make waves." She wiped off Danny's mouth with his bib. "Unfortunately, not making waves taught me a hard lesson." She turned to Paisley. "If there are no waves, you never get anywhere."

The analogy was so true. Without waves, you

were dead in the water. That's certainly how Paisley felt. Like she was treading in a still pool, trying to keep from sinking.

"How did you learn to voice your feelings?" she asked.

Adeline thought for a moment. "I guess I got tired of not taking charge of my own life."

After everyone finished eating, Shane volunteered to take Henry back to the stables to see Glory Boy. Paisley thought she would have nothing to do, but she soon learned there was plenty to do on a working ranch. When she finished helping with the lunch dishes, Gretchen asked her to help bake pies for Nasty Jack's. After that, she helped Adeline study for a test she was taking online the following day. She was surprised the busy mother, wife, and manager of Buckinghorse Palace found time to go back to school to become a veterinarian. But Adeline seemed to handle it well and it made Paisley wonder if it would be possible for her to work at Nasty Jack's, take care of Henry, and study for her nursing examine.

Dinner was as chaotic and enjoyable as lunch. Once she helped with the dishes, she took Henry upstairs to get ready for bed. She should be exhausted. But regardless of how comfortable the mattress was and how soothing Henry's even breathing, she still had trouble getting to sleep. She was no longer scared. In fact, she felt safer than she'd felt in a long time. Nothing like sleeping in the tall tower of a castle surrounded by good people to make a person feel safe.

Just not tired.

Giving up on sleep, she climbed out of bed and moved to the window that looked out on the Kingmans' impressive garden. Paisley had walked past the English-style garden when she'd been to the ranch for Everly and Chance's wedding, but she hadn't gotten a chance to walk through it. Now, she had the overwhelming desire to walk along the stone path that wound through the profusion of flowers and shrubs. Of course, she couldn't. Not with Jonathan's threat hanging over her head.

But the more she looked at the garden, the stronger the urge became. And what would it hurt to take a quick walk? Jonathan had no clue where she was staying. Since she had only arrived at the ranch that day, none of the ranch hands would have had the chance to spread the news to the people in town.

Turning from the window, she headed to the closet and slipped on a pair of running shoes and a sweater. The entire house was dark and quiet as she stepped into the hallway and made her way downstairs. In the kitchen, she cringed when she ran into a chair and the legs loudly scraped across the floor. She was more careful as she moved through the mudroom and out the back door.

The temperature had warmed drastically over the last week—which was normal for winter in Texas. You never knew whether you were going to get freezing sleet or balmy breezes. Tonight, there was only a slight chill in the air.

Paisley wrapped her sweater closer around her

as she walked down the path toward the garden gate. The garden was as magical as the castle. The quaint stone cottage Lily and Stetson lived in sat to the left of the garden. Fairy lights had been strung up in the branches of the trees and the scent of fertile soil and spring hung heavy in the air.

Paisley took her time strolling along the path, stopping to admire the flowers or read the names of the championship thoroughbreds on the bronze horse statues placed throughout the garden. At the end of the path, she came to a set of brick steps that led down. When she reached the bottom, she discovered a row of tall shrubbery with a break in the front. She stepped through it and realized it was a labyrinth.

She felt like a kid as she rounded each leafy corner. It wasn't until she was well into the maze that she realized how large the labyrinth was. Her carefree inner child was replaced with her commonsense adult and she started to worry she might not find her way out.

She turned to go back the way she'd come when she heard the sound of trickling water. She followed the sound to a hidden break in the shrubs. When she stepped through, her breath caught at the sight that greeted her.

It was a hidden garden. A beautiful hidden garden with a mosaic tile fountain surrounded by lush, green lawns. The fountain was lit not only by lights, but also by moonlight. The water looked like liquid silver as it flowed from the top tier of the fountain and splashed to the pool below.

No longer concerned about getting lost in the maze, she moved to the fountain and sat down on the edge. Beneath the surface of the water, she could see the coins that glistened at the bottom—no doubt wishes the Kingmans had made over the years. There were a lot of wishes. She had to wonder what a family who seemed to have everything would wish for.

"Paisley?"

The husky voice caused her to startle. She turned to see Hayden's tall shadowy form standing in the break of the hedge. Her peaceful moment was gone, replaced with the nervous energy she always felt when Hayden was near. She got to her feet and pulled her sweater closer around her.

"What are you doing here?"

"I heard someone moving around in the kitchen and came out of my bedroom to investigate."

He slept in the castle? There went her plan to stay away from him. "I thought you slept in the bunkhouse."

"I did, but . . . I got promoted. With the promotion came a room in the house. What are you doing here?"

"I couldn't sleep and thought a walk would help."

He studied her. He wasn't wearing a hat and his blue eyes reflected the moonlight. "Jonathan can't harm you here." He stepped closer and lifted a hand as if to touch her. She took a step back, her bare legs bumping into the cold stone of the fountain edge. But he didn't touch her. He just held open his hand. Resting over the healing cut in his palm was a dime. "Go ahead. Make a wish. Contrary to what you believe, I have another one."

Her face heated when she realized what he was referring to. "I'm sorry," she said. "I shouldn't have said that."

He shrugged as he lowered his hand. "It's pretty much the truth. I am a saddle tramp."

An image of him calming Royal Duke popped into her head. The stallion had been huge and angry looking. Paisley had been terrified just watching Hayden holding the reins of the rearing, fighting beast. But Hayden hadn't shown any signs of fear. He had soothed the animal with soft words and a firm hand. It had been amazing to watch . . . and eye opening.

"Obviously, being a saddle tramp takes talent. You're extremely good with angry horses. I thought for sure Royal Duke was going to trample you."

He grinned. It was annoying how just a flash of teeth could make Paisley's knees weak. "You mean Spunky. And he wasn't angry. He was just scared. Most people get the two confused."

"But not you."

His eyes drilled into hers. "Call it a sixth sense. I know when someone's angry and when they're just running scared."

She knew he wasn't just talking about the horse. "I guess you think because I came to the ranch that I'm running scared."

"No. I think you came here to protect your son." He hesitated. "But I get the feeling you want to run right now. At first, I thought it was all men that made you skittish. But you don't act skittish with Chance, or Shane, or any of the Kingmans. Just me. Why is that?"

They were moving into dangerous territory. Territory she refused to even think about, let alone discuss with Hayden. Because he was right. It wasn't all men who made her feel all jumpy and restless like a stranger in her own skin.

And she wasn't about to let him know that.

Completely avoiding the question, she turned away from him and looked at the fountain. "You aren't seriously going to call that beautiful horse Spunky, are you?"

He hesitated as if he wasn't going to accept the subject change. But, thankfully, he did. "Why not? Just because you're beautiful doesn't mean you can't have a cute nickname. I bet you were called something cute when you were a kid." Before she could get over him calling her beautiful, he continued in a teasing voice. "Let me guess. Your nickname was Scooter."

She glanced at him. "Scooter?"

"Yeah, because you loved to ride your scooter with your blond braids flying."

She shook her head. "No. I didn't have a scooter. I had a bicycle that I rarely rode."

"Ahhh, so you were a bookworm. Bookie? Wormie?"

"Wormie? That's not cute. That's disgusting."

He rubbed the scruff on his jaw. She couldn't

help wondering if it felt rough or soft. "You've got a point." He glanced at her. "Poppins because you were constantly popping up when folks least expected it? Or what about Chubs because you had a little extra baby fat as a kid?"

"No and no. I didn't pop and I was always skinny as a stick."

"Skinny Minnie? Bones?"

She couldn't keep from laughing at his silliness. She stopped when she noticed him studying her. "What?"

"Nothing. You just have a nice laugh. You should use it more."

Her smile faded. "Pea. The only nickname I had was Pea."

He crinkled his nose. "And pee's not disgusting?"

"Not like that kind of pee. Pea like in peas and carrots. Everly called me that when she was a toddler and couldn't pronounce Paisley."

He grinned. "See, I knew you had a cute nickname." He held out the dime. "Now make a wish, Pea."

She hesitated for just a moment before she took the dime. It was warm from his skin and seemed to burn a hole in her palm as her fingers closed around it. He watched her intently as she closed her eyes and made a wish for Henry to grow up happy and safe.

Then she tossed the coin.

She opened her eyes in time to see the dime hitting the top tier of the fountain and bouncing back at them.

Hayden reached out and caught it. He looked at her and grinned. "I guess that means I get your wish, Pea."

"It most certainly does not." She reached for his hand to take back the dime, but he held it over his head.

"Nope. I caught your wish, I'm keeping it." He closed his eyes and tossed the coin. She didn't see a splash, but she didn't doubt for a second that the dime had hit the water. Hayden was too good at everything he did to miss. Anger filled her and made her do something she had never done in her life.

She socked a boy.

She socked him hard in the arm.

"That was my wish!"

Hayden's eyes widened and he stared back at her with stunned shock. She was just as stunned. "Oh. I'm so—" Before she could apologize, he laughed. Not just a little chuckle, but a deep out-and-out belly laugh that was more annoying than him stealing her wish.

"Hitting people is not funny," she grumbled.

"I wouldn't call that a hit. I've swatted at gnats harder." He turned his shoulder to her. "Go ahead. Punch me again, but this time put your weight behind it."

"I am not going to punch you again. I am not some rowdy cowboy who enjoys fighting. I suppose this is how you taught Henry to punch that poor little boy in his preschool class."

The smile faded from Hayden's face as he turned to her. "Henry punched someone at school?"

"As if you didn't know. He said you were the one who told him that a man has to stand up for what he wants."

"I wasn't talking about hitting anyone. I was talking about him not giving up on Brooklyn Ann just because Brendan liked her too." He stared at her. "You thought I would teach a child to hit?" When she didn't answer, he shook his head. "Not all men are like Jonathan, Paisley. You need to figure that out. Your son is going to grow up to be a man and he doesn't need a mama who can't trust him." He turned and headed for the break in the hedges.

When he was gone, Paisley sat down on the ledge of the fountain and sighed. Was he right? Had she let her relationship with Jonathan color how she viewed all men? Including her son? She thought Henry had pulled away from her, but what if she was the one who had pulled away from him? She had been worried that he had his father's genes. Did she just see him as another man trying to control her life?

And, sadly, he *did* control it. All he had to do was throw a fit and she usually gave him anything he wanted. She hadn't even disciplined him for running out in the street or hitting the boy at school. Instead of acting like a parent, she'd been acting like a scared woman worried about losing her son's love. So, basically, she had given Henry control. Just like she'd done with Jonathan and her parents. She'd been so worried about losing their love that she'd lost herself.

Hayden was right. She *was* running scared. And not from him. Or Jonathan. Or Henry.

She was running from herself and her own insecurities.

All this time, she had blamed her parents and Jonathan for her not having her own life. But it wasn't their fault. It was hers. They had learned how to get what they wanted. Now she needed to learn how to get what she wanted.

As the truth dawned, something shiny on the ledge of the fountain caught her attention. When she reached out and picked it up, moonlight reflected on the silver dime.

Hayden hadn't stolen her wish after all.

Closing her eyes, she tossed the coin into the fountain. But this time, she didn't make a wish. She made a vow. A vow to become the type of woman who would make her own wishes come true.

CHAPTER TEN

HAYDEN DIDN'T GO back to the house after he left the labyrinth. As upset as he was with Paisley for thinking he was the type of man to tell a child to use his fists to dispute a problem, he wasn't about to let her roam around the ranch at night by herself. He waited in the shadows of the garden until she was safely back in the house before he headed to bed.

His room was a far cry from the bunkhouse. It was spacious and nicely decorated with a king-sized bed that had a firm mattress and soft pillows. He should have fallen asleep easily. But instead, he lay there thinking about Paisley.

The moment he had seen her standing by the fountain with her hair glowing in the moonlight like wild moonbeams, his brain had conjured up a fantasy of waking up every morning and finding her standing in a cozy kitchen wearing those flannel pajamas and that oversized sweater. When she saw him, she'd walk right over to him and loop her arms around his neck and press those soft lips against his. Right there in the kitchen, he'd strip off that sweater and those pajamas and find her warm and willing.

Except she wasn't warm and willing.

She was cold and distant.

Stetson's words had given him hope that maybe Paisley held some kind of attraction for him. But tonight had proven otherwise. She wasn't attracted to him. She didn't even trust him. His mama had taught him early on that trust was a crucial part of any relationship. Hayden had learned the lesson well and had worked hard to be a trustworthy person. Not only with people, but also with animals. It stung badly that Paisley thought he was the type of person who would teach a child to hit.

And it didn't matter. Even if she did trust him, a relationship with Paisley would never work. They were two completely different people. Paisley was beautiful, college educated, and used to living in a big house with nice things. He was average looking, had barely made it through high school, and only had a small savings account and a big dream of one day owning his own horse ranch.

Paisley didn't even like horses.

Although Glory Boy had gotten her to smile. But smiling at an adorable colt was one thing. Living on a horse ranch something else entirely. And Hayden couldn't give up his dream. Horses were in his blood and always had been. He didn't understand why until he'd come to the Kingman Ranch. Now he knew that he came from a horse-loving family. Knowing his heritage had made him want a ranch even more.

It had also changed his dreams. At one time, all he'd wanted was a small ranch with a few thoroughbred horses. But after seeing what was possible with hard work and determination, his dream had gotten much bigger. Now, he wanted to run a large breeding ranch with a house big enough for a family. A family that argued and fought, but always had each other's backs. And maybe it wasn't just the Kingmans who had changed his dream. Paisley had played a part in it too. Even if she didn't return his love, she'd made him realize that true love did exist.

Hopefully, he'd find it again. Next time, with a woman who could return it.

After hours of tossing and turning, he finally fell asleep. When he woke, bright sunlight streamed in through the window. He'd obviously overslept—something you couldn't do in a crowded bunkhouse with a bunch of noisy cowboys. Normally, he wouldn't be worried about oversleeping. Sunday was usually his day off. But today the Kingmans planned to gather the winter calves for branding and Hayden had told Buck he would help. That was if they weren't already gone.

He rolled to his back and started to get up when he saw Batman sitting cross-legged on the foot of his bed. The black mask was a little crooked, but still scary.

"Shit!"

At Hayden's exclamation, Henry pushed the Batman mask to the top of his head and grinned.

"It's just me, Hay. And don't worry. I won't tell Mama you said a bad word."

Hayden rubbed the sleep from his eyes as he sat up. "What are you doing here, partner?"

"Potts told me that you mobed into Bucking-horse Palace just like me and Mama did so I came to see you. Why didn't you want to sleep in the bunkhouse with the rest of the cowboys, Hay? Sleeping in the bunkhouse would be fun." Henry glanced down at his bare chest. "Is it 'cause you don't habe pajamas like the other cowboys?"

"Cowboys usually don't wear pajamas, partner."

"What do you wear?" Before Hayden could stop him, Henry pulled back the sheet. His eyes widened and his mouth formed a big O as Hayden quickly grabbed the sheet and covered himself back up.

"Okay, Henry James, we need to get a few things straight right now. First, you don't show up in someone's room without an invitation. Second, you don't go around grabbing people's covers. That's not good manners."

"But why do you sleep naked, Hay? Don't you get cold?"

Before Hayden could answer, Paisley peeked her head in the open door. "There you are. What are you doing—" Her words cut off when she saw Hayden. Her gaze lowered to his bare chest and her cheeks flamed a bright pink before she quickly looked away. Just not quick enough. All it had taken for a morning erection to make an appearance was the feel of those spring-meadow eyes on his bare skin. He grabbed the comforter he'd kicked to the foot of the bed and pulled it over his lap to hide the evidence.

"Oh, pardon me," she apologized. "I didn't realize this was your room." With her eyes still averted, she reached a hand toward Henry. "Come on, Henry. You shouldn't have disrupted Hayden's sleep. Especially on his only day off."

"I didn't 'rupt Hay's sleep. I sat right here and waited until he woke up. You know what, Mama?"

Hayden knew what was coming. He tried to stop the kid, but Henry yelled out before he could.

"Hay sleeps naked!"

Paisley's eyes flashed back to him and her mouth formed the same *O* as her son's had. Hayden blushed like a thirteen-year-old kid and tried to explain. "In case you're thinking I ran around naked in front of your son, I didn't. He pulled the covers off to see what cowboys wore. And for the record, I couldn't find any clean boxers last night. I don't normally sleep . . ." He let the sentence drift off, as his face grew even hotter.

"Can I sleep naked, Mama?" Henry asked. "Can I? I promise I won't get cold."

Paisley pulled her attention away from Hayden and turned to Henry. "No, you may not."

Henry jumped to his feet and started bouncing up and down on the bed. "But I want to sleep naked like cowboys do! I want to sleep naked! And you're a mean mama if you won't—" He cut off when Paisley picked him up and set him down in front of her. When she spoke, it wasn't with her usual tone. This tone was stern and no-nonsense.

"That is enough, Henry James Stanford. When I tell you no, it means no. From now on, every time you throw a tantrum, I'm going to take away one of your toys. Starting with this one." She slipped the Batman mask off his head. Which really sent Henry into a tantrum.

"No-o-o! Not my Batman mask!"

"Keep it up and your new Tonka dump truck will be next."

Henry stopped jumping and slammed his mouth closed. He glared at her for a long moment before he burst into tears. Hayden waited for Paisley to cave. She didn't. Instead, she turned to Hayden.

"Do cowboys throw tantrums when they don't get their way, Hayden?"

Henry cut off crying and stared at Hayden with tearful eyes.

"No, ma'am," Hayden said. "There's no place for tantrum throwing on a ranch. It would startle the animals. Not to mention cowboys always respect their mamas."

She looked back at Henry. "Hmm? That's what I thought."

Henry sniffed and spoke in a wobbly voice. "I 'spect my mama."

"Throwing fits and running off without telling me where you're going is not respecting your mother," Paisley said.

His lip puffed out. "But I'm not a cowboy. Cowboys know how to ride horses. And you won't let Hay teach me."

Hayden figured Paisley would start talking about Henry being too young to ride. Surprisingly, she didn't. "Well, maybe I would change my mind about you being too young, if you stopped acting like a tantrum-throwing baby."

Henry's eyes widened. "I'm not a baby!"

"Then stop acting like one. Now go get dressed. Potts has breakfast almost ready and we need to eat before we head to church."

"But I don't want to go to—" He cut off when Paisley sent him a warning look. "Yes, ma'am," he grumbled before he glanced at Hayden. "See you later, Hay."

"See ya, partner."

When he was gone, Paisley released her breath in a long sigh. He couldn't help giving her a little encouragement.

"You did good."

She shook her head as she continued to look at the empty doorway. "If I'd done good, he wouldn't be a spoiled brat."

"He's a good kid who just needs a firm hand. It looks like you found one."

She turned to him. "I'm sorry he woke you this morning." She hesitated. "Especially when I woke you last night."

"No problem. I don't need a lot of sleep."

He figured she'd leave, but instead she continued to stand there, her gaze wandering around the room. He was glad he hadn't unpacked all his things yet. He wasn't exactly a neat person. While she took in the room, he took in her. She was dressed in a silky-looking top that draped over

the slopes of her breasts and a beige skirt that fell
a few inches above her knees. Her legs looked
twice as long in the high heels she had on. She
wore makeup, but not too much. Just enough to
accentuate the meadow green of her eyes and full
curves of her soft lips. She'd curled her hair and
it fell in a tumbling mass of sunshine around her
shoulders.

Classy came to mind when he looked at her.
Stunningly beautiful and classy.

Just looking at her made him ache. Not just in a
place that had him adjusting the blankets over his
lap, but also in his soul. Words he had no business
saying pushed to get out.

He held them in.

"Was there something else?"

She stared back at him with eyes that didn't
hold annoyance or disgust like they usually did.
They were a clear green a man could easily get
lost in.

"I wanted to thank you."

"For what?" he asked.

"For saving Henry. I should've thanked you
sooner. But when Kitty showed up with the
divorce papers, I got a little distracted. Anyway, I
just wanted you to know how much I appreciate
you saving my son." She hesitated. "And I know
you didn't teach him to hit . . . it was stupid of
me to think that. You're right. I have been thinking all men are like Jonathan. And that's not fair.
Especially to Henry."

"It's understandable," he said. "A horse gets bit

by a dog, it's only normal for that horse to get all riled up every time it's around any dog."

She tipped her head. "And I'm the horse in that scenario?"

"More like a beautiful filly."

She blushed and looked away. "Well, I need to stop getting riled up and start having a little courage."

"Courage?" Hayden stared at her. "You don't think it takes courage to leave your life and start over? Pardon my language, but that takes a hel-luva lot of courage, Paisley. Not many women in your situation could've done what you did."

She stood there looking at him for a long moment before she smiled. It wasn't like the other smiles he'd seen. Those had just been smiles. This smile felt like it was just for him. It caused some-thing to flicker to life deep down inside him. Something that hadn't been there before.

Hope.

"Well, I better go check on Henry. I'm sure he didn't listen to a word I said and is chattering away to Potts." She turned for the door, but then stopped and looked back at him. "You tricked me."

"Excuse me?"

"You didn't steal my wish."

"I would never steal your wish, Paisley," he said sincerely. The only thing he wanted was for all her wishes to come true. "So I'm assuming you hit the water on your next try."

"I did. But I didn't make a wish. I've decided

I'm through wishing for things." She hesitated. "It's time I started fighting for what I want."

She gifted him with another smile before she swept out of the room.

As Hayden stared at the empty doorway, he couldn't help wondering what it would be like to have Paisley fight for him.

CHAPTER ELEVEN

"PAISE! WHAT ARE you doing here?"
Everly hurried across the church parking
lot before Paisley could even get out of her car.
"I thought we agreed that you wouldn't leave the
ranch until the divorce was final and we knew
Jonathan wasn't going to do anything crazy."

Paisley got out and closed her door. "I gave
up working at the bar and taking Henry to preschool. I'm not giving up church."

"It's only for a couple weeks, Paise. If you want
spiritual guidance, Chance could come out to the
ranch."

"I'm not having Chance come all the way out
to the ranch. Jonathan isn't going to show up in
broad daylight in the middle of a church service."
She opened Henry's door. He had been quiet for
most of the ride into town, probably because he
was still mad at her for getting after him. But he
immediately perked up when he saw Everly.

"Hey, Aunt Eberly! Guess what? Cowboys
sleep naked."

"And just how do you know that?" Everly
unbuckled his booster seat and helped him out.

"'Cause I saw Hayden's wienie. And you know what? It's much bigger than mine."

Everly straightened and stared at Paisley. "He what?"

"It was purely by accident," Paisley said. She gave her son a stern look. "Henry pulled the covers off Hayden."

"And exactly why was Hayden sleeping naked in your bed, Paise?"

It was Paisley's turn to be shocked. "He wasn't in my bed! He was in his bed. In his room."

"Well, that's too bad. I thought that maybe my sister had decided to have a little slumber party."

"A slumber party!" Henry squealed, jumping up and down. "Can we habe a slumber party with Hayden, Mama? Can we? Can we?"

Just the thought of having a slumber party with Hayden brought up an image of how he had looked that morning.

Damn good.

His hair had been mussed and his eyes sleepy . . . and sexy. And so was his layer of dark beard. Then there was his body. It was tanned and broad with the kind of muscles you could only get from hard work. His chest and arms were a 3D collage of fist-sized knots and ropey ridges that fit together like an intricate puzzle of hot cowboy. It had been a struggle to pull her gaze away. She had never thought she'd feel desire for a man again, but she couldn't deny she had felt it for Hayden. The thought of him being completely naked under the covers had made her entire body flush with heat.

And still did.

"No," she said a little sterner than she'd planned. She wasn't just talking to Henry. She was talking to herself. "We cannot have a slumber party with Hayden. Ever." When Henry got the obstinate look on his face that said a tantrum was imminent, she quickly continued, "Remember what Hayden said about cowboys throwing tantrums."

Henry immediately stopped jumping and sulked. "Yes, ma'am."

Everly shot Paisley a curious look, but she didn't say anything until after they had dropped Henry off in the Sunday school room. "Okay, so just what is going on with Hayden?"

"What do you mean?"

"First, you act like you can't stand the guy and now you're letting Henry hang out in his room and are using him as a threat to keep Henry from throwing tantrums."

"I didn't let Henry hang out in his room. He went there without me knowing . . . and uninvited. I'm sure Hayden didn't want to be woken up by a five-year-old in a Batman mask. And I'm not using him as a threat." She hesitated. "Okay, maybe I am. But being a cowboy like Hayden is the only thing that seems to motivate Henry to behave."

Everly raised her hands. "Hallelujah! It's about time you stopped spoiling that kid because you feel guilty about taking him away from his home."

"I still feel guilty. I took him from everything he knew. But I've come to terms with the fact that it was something I had to do—for his safety and mine. And now I have to figure out how to give Henry a home just as nice, but in a safe environment."

Everly hooked her arm through Paisley's. "We will, Paise. Once everything gets settled, we'll figure out what to do next." It was sweet of Everly to want to help her. But Paisley knew it was something she needed to figure out on her own. It was scary, but she was through letting fear paralyze her.

The Sunday service was enjoyable. Mrs. Moody made an announcement on the upcoming church Easter egg hunt and asked for volunteers to fill eggs. Then Miss Kitty got up and asked for people to donate all their old formals for the Prom Dress Fundraiser the Cursed Ladies' Auxiliary Club was doing. After that, Everly led the congregation in hymns and Chance gave a humorous and thought-provoking sermon about spring being a time of renewal—a time to let go of the old and welcome the new. He spoke straight to Paisley's heart. It was time to let go of the past and move forward.

When church was over, Paisley went in search of Mrs. Moody to tell her that she'd be happy to help fill Easter eggs. The she headed toward the stairs to pick up Henry from Sunday school. Everly had invited them over for dinner and she knew Henry would be thrilled. Not only because he loved Everly and Chance, but also because he would get to see their three kittens, Flounder, Sebastian, and Scuttle. Once Paisley found them a home, she planned to get him his own pet.

Hopefully, he wouldn't want a horse.

"Where's Henry?"

Hester's voice had Paisley turning and smiling at the older woman. But her smile faded when she saw Hester's concerned face. "He's in Sunday school class. I was just going to get him. Are you okay, Hester?"

Hester's worried expression didn't change. "You need to get him now and take him straight back to the ranch."

Paisley didn't ask why. With her heart beating overtime, she hurried up the stairs. When she got to the Sunday school room, the young woman who taught the class looked surprised to see her.

"But his father already came and got him."

Paisley's heart felt like it stopped beating and dropped to her feet. "His father?"

The woman nodded. "I thought it would be okay. Henry knew him. He called him Daddy."

It was hard to speak through the ball of fear in her throat. "Where did they go?"

The young woman grew concerned. "I didn't ask. Is everything okay?"

Without answering, Paisley turned and headed for the stairs. She frantically searched through the people crowded in the vestibule, even though she knew Jonathan and Henry wouldn't be there.

"He wasn't there, was he?"

She turned to Hester with tears in her eyes. "What did you see, Hessy? Did you see where Jonathan took him?"

Hester shook her head as she rubbed the crystal hanging around her neck. "All I see is the same darkness I saw the night Jonathan showed up here."

Paisley's voice shook with fear. "If he hurts Henry, I swear I'll kill him."

Hester took her hand and squeezed it. "He's not going to hurt Henry. Like I said before, a courageous queen will rise up and destroy Jonathan's power."

Paisley wished she could believe her. But she wasn't about to bet her son's life on one of Hester's visions. She pulled out her cellphone to call the sheriff. Before she could dial 911, it rang. She didn't recognize the number, but she answered anyway. Every nerve in her body came to attention when she heard Jonathan's voice.

"Hey, sweetheart. Guess who?"

She didn't even try to keep the anger from her voice. "Where is Henry?"

"He's right here. You want to talk to him?"

A second later, Henry's voice came through the receiver. "Hey, Ma–ma." The wobble in his voice told her that he was scared. She tried to keep the fear out of her own voice.

"Hey, sweet boy. Are you okay?"

"I didn't want to leabe church with Daddy, Mama. I told him that you wouldn't like it, but he made me anyway."

"It's okay, baby. Can you tell Mama where you are? I'll come get you."

"I'm—" He cut off and Jonathan spoke.

"I don't think you need to know where we are when you're still in church surrounded by all your new friends. If you want to see Henry, you need to keep your mouth shut and walk out the door. Alone. And right now while we're still on the phone."

Paisley glanced at Hester. "Okay. I won't talk to anyone. I'm leaving the church now." She mouthed the words *Call the sheriff* before she turned for the door. When she stepped outside, she searched the parking lot. She didn't see Jonathan's SUV, but he could have easily gotten a new car like he'd gotten a new cellphone number. "Where are you?"

"Don't worry about where I am. Just get in your car and head south out of town. I'll be right behind you."

She glanced around the entire time she walked to her car, but she didn't see Jonathan or Henry. But they had to be somewhere close. She was right. As soon as she pulled out of the parking lot, a black Jeep started following her. It was too far away to see who was driving, but she knew it was Jonathan.

"Where am I going?" she asked. The Bluetooth in the Range Rover had taken over and Jonathan's voice came through the speakers.

"Just drive. I'll tell you when to pull over."

"I'll do whatever you ask, Jonathan. But if you hurt Henry . . ."

"You'll what?" His voice became low and angry. "Don't ever threaten me, bitch. Do you hear me? Ever."

Her stomach tightened with fear. But this time, she wasn't scared for herself. She was scared for Henry. If she wanted to keep him safe, she had to do everything in her power to keep Jonathan calm.

"I'm sorry. I would never threaten you. I'm just a little worried about Henry."

"You always worry about Henry more than you do me. That's why you left me, isn't it? You left me because I threatened your kid."

It was what he called Henry. Not his son. Or their child. But her kid. It still broke her heart. Henry deserved so much more than a father who couldn't even acknowledge him. Paisley wanted to tell Jonathan that, but she couldn't. Not when he had Henry.

"Henry wasn't the reason I left you, Jonathan," she said. "I left you because I refused to take your beatings anymore."

"Beatings? I never beat you. I just gave you a few slaps. And only because you refuse to listen."

The lie was so outrageous she almost laughed. But laughing at Jonathan had always set him off. So she tried a different tactic. "You're right. I've never been good at listening. But I'm listening now. What do you want, Jonathan?"

"What do I want? You know what I want. Now pull off the highway at the next turnoff."

The next turnoff was nothing but a dirt road. As she headed down it, she started to get worried. When they were on the main highway, it would have been easy for the sheriff to find them. Now, she didn't even know where they were. Although they had to be close to the Kingman Ranch. The Kingmans owned most of the land south of Cursed.

The thought had her reaching for her phone and texting Shane.

need help on dirt road just south of cursed heading west She noticed a dilapidated old shed of some kind with faded red paint and added, past old shed with red paint

"What the fuck are you doing?"

Jonathan's voice startled her and she almost dropped her phone. She pushed send and placed it back in the cup holder before she spoke.

"I'm doing exactly what you told me to do. I'm driving down this road."

"And texting for help. Pull over! Pull over now!"

"Don't yell at my mama!" Henry yelled.

"Shut up! I'll fuckin' yell at whoever I want to yell at."

Fear for Henry had her quickly pulling off the road. She jumped out of the car, and as soon as Jonathan stopped, she had the back door open. Henry wasn't buckled in and flew straight into her arms.

"Mama!"

She hugged him close as tears filled her eyes. "Hey, baby." She drew back and looked at him. "You okay?"

Tears streaked his cheeks. "Uh-huh. But I want to go home."

"See," Jonathan said. "He wants to go back to Mesaville."

"No!" Henry yelled. "I want to go home to the Kingman Ranch."

She wiped at his tears. "Okay, baby. But we

need to take care of something first." She set him down. "Go get in the Range Rover and I'll be there in a second."

He started to follow her instructions, but Jonathan stepped in front of him and grabbed his arm. "No. He's not going anywhere but back in my car. And neither are you." His gaze narrowed on her. "You're my wife. You will always be my wife."

"And if I don't want to be your wife?"

There was a long pause before he spoke. "I think I can change your mind." He picked Henry up and tossed him into the front seat of the Jeep before he turned on Paisley. She knew what was going to happen before he even lifted his hand. His fist struck her on the cheek and she went down. She lay there dazed until Henry screamed.

"Don't you hit my mama!"

Paisley glanced up to see Henry hurling himself out of the car at Jonathan. The attack must have taken him by surprise because he stumbled back and tripped over a rock, landing hard on his butt as Henry pummeled him with his tiny fists . . . until Jonathan grabbed him and threw him. Henry landed hard on the ground with a yelp of pain.

Something rose up inside of Paisley. Something wild and feral. It flooded her mind with a red haze of anger that's only focus was the animal who had just hurt her son.

Paisley's hand closed around a jagged rock on the ground. With a low growl, she got to her feet and attacked. She dove at Jonathan, knocking him back to the ground. Then she raised the rock like a knife and slashed down. She only grazed his cheek before he brought up his arm and knocked the rock out of her hand. But that didn't stop her from using her nails to claw at his face.

"I'm going to kill you, you bitch," he yelled.

She sank her nails into the soft flesh of his cheeks. "Not if I kill you first."

He hit her, but she didn't even feel it. She felt . . . invincible. Powerful. She couldn't lose this fight. She wouldn't lose this fight. She didn't know how long she would have kept scratching and punching if Henry hadn't yelled out.

"Hey! Hey!"

At first, she thought he was trying to get her attention. But when she glanced over at him, he was standing and waving his arms over his head at something behind them. She looked and saw a horse and rider approaching at a fast gallop. There were other horses and riders behind him, but it was Hayden who reached them first. He swung down from the saddle before the horse had even come to a full stop. Just like a cowboy hero. And like a hero, he didn't need to ask what was going on. He just walked over and lifted Paisley off Jonathan and set her on her feet before he knocked Jonathan out with one punch.

"Hay!" Henry raced toward Hayden and jumped into his arms.

Hayden caught him and held him close as he looked at Paisley. "You okay?"

She had spent her life saying she was fine when she wasn't. But this time when she said it, she meant it. "I'm fine."

She *was* fine. She felt better than she had felt in a long time. Jonathan started coming to and sat up. She no longer feared him. In fact, she just pitied him. He needed help, but she couldn't help him. She could only help herself and her son.

"I'm getting a divorce, Jonathan. Nothing you do will stop me. It's over. Do you hear me? Over."

As she turned away, she knew it was.

CHAPTER TWELVE

HAYDEN WAS PISSED. If Henry and Paisley hadn't been there, he would have done a lot more than just punch Jonathan. He would have beaten him within an inch of his life.

But Paisley and Henry *were* there, and both of them looked like they had been through enough hell. Henry was sobbing his little heart out in Paisley's arms and Paisley looked like she was seconds away from joining him. Which had Hayden clenching his fists and glaring at Jonathan who still sat on the ground. He must have read Hayden's rage because he looked terrified. He looked even more scared when the other cowboys rode up.

Hayden had been separating calves with Stetson, Shane, Buck, and Wolfe when Shane had gotten the text from Paisley. Everyone thought Paisley had just had car trouble. But Hayden's gut had known it was something more. Especially when Shane texted her back and she didn't reply. Hayden knew exactly where the old faded feed shed was and he wasted no time heading in that direction. When he saw the black Jeep parked behind Paisley's Range Rover, his fear had grown. He had ridden faster than he had ever ridden in his life, praying the entire time.

He expected to find Jonathan abusing Paisley and Henry. He had not expected to find Paisley beating up on her husband. She'd done some damage to Jonathan's face and his jaw was swelling from where Hayden had hit him. Still, it wasn't enough. As soon as Paisley and Henry were gone, Hayden intended to mete out more justice.

"What happened?" Stetson asked as he swung down from his horse.

"It seems Paisley's estranged husband showed up to threaten her in person," Hayden said. "Could you drive her and Henry back to the house while I . . . make things clear to Jonathan?"

Stetson glanced over at Paisley and Henry before he looked back at Hayden. "I don't think that's a good idea."

Wolfe moved his horse closer as his gaze narrowed on Jonathan. "I think it's a great idea. In fact, I'll be happy to stay and help you make things clear, Hay."

"I doubt Hayden needs your help, big brother," Buck said. "Especially when it looks like someone already got the best of this jackass. But if you don't mind, Hay, I'd like to stay and watch . . . you make things clear."

"No one is making anything clear but the sheriff." Stetson sent Hayden a warning look. "Now head on back to the ranch, Hayden. I'll handle this."

Hayden knew Stetson was his boss, but this was

one time he couldn't follow an order. "I'm not leaving until justice has been served. If you fire me for it, so be it."

Stetson went to say something, but Paisley cut in.

"I don't want anyone going to jail because they feel like they have to defend me. I can defend myself." She sent Hayden a hard look. "Something I think I proved before you got here. I'm fine. Just fine. Now if y'all will excuse me, I'm taking my son back to the ranch."

Hayden might have let her go if he hadn't noticed the glint of tears in her eyes and the wobble in her legs as she carried Henry to the car. She was in no condition to drive. He glanced at Jonathan and growled in a low voice.

"Fuck with her or Henry again and there will be no place you can hide. You understand? No place on God's green earth." He hurried after Paisley.

She wasn't happy about it.

"I told you that I don't need anyone to drive us back to the ranch."

"I know you don't, but I think Henry needs the comfort of his mama's arms right now. If you're driving, you can't give him that."

She hesitated for only a second before she nodded.

He took the side roads back to Buckinghorse Palace. They didn't talk. The only sound in the car was Henry's soft sobs. Hayden wanted to say something to make him feel better, but he knew there were no words that could make up for having a father who didn't care about you. It was something you had to come to terms with on your own.

But he couldn't help wanting to give some comfort to the little guy. He remembered how soothing it was when Jimmy sang old country songs to him when he'd been a kid. So he turned on the radio and searched through the stations until he found Dolly Parton singing about a coat of many colors. He sang along until Henry finally quieted. He didn't realize Henry had fallen asleep until they got to the ranch and he was helping Paisley out of the car.

"Stress can sure tucker you out," he said. Paisley nodded as she adjusted Henry in her arms. She looked tuckered out too. "Here," he said. "Why don't you let me carry him up to your room?"

She opened her mouth and he thought for sure she was going to refuse the offer, but then she closed it again and handed Henry to him.

There was something soothing and blissful about holding a sleeping kid in your arms. Henry's warm body melted into his with such complete trust that it brought tears to Hayden's eyes. As he carried him into the house, he had the overwhelming desire to take on the world for Henry. He wanted to protect him and teach him and watch him grow into a good man.

But he didn't have that right. All he could do was love and protect him for this moment.

"I got you, partner," he said in a low whisper. "I got you."

Since he had never been upstairs in Buckinghorse Palace, he let Paisley lead the way. The guest room was just as nicely furnished as his, but twice as big with an en suite bathroom and large windows that looked out on the garden.

Henry didn't even rouse as Hayden laid him on the bed. Paisley removed his boots without waking him—something only a mama could do—and pulled a throw blanket over him before giving him a kiss. She remained there for a long moment with her lips pressed to her son's forehead. Hayden figured she was thanking God for not letting anything happen to him. He would have left if he hadn't noticed her shoulders shaking. The soft sob broke his heart.

"Hey, now." When he placed a comforting hand on her shoulder, she turned and fell into his arms, muffling her sobs against his chest. Again, he had the overwhelming desire to protect. He held her close and repeated what he'd told Henry. "I got you, Pea. I got you." It didn't seem to help. Her sobs grew louder. When Henry started to rouse, Hayden shuffled her back toward the bathroom and pulled the door closed behind them.

"Just let it go." He pressed a kiss to the top of her head. "Just let it go."

She seemed to have a lot to let go. The front of his western shirt was soaked by the time she quieted. And still he held her. If this was the only time he was going to get to do it, he was in no hurry to let her go.

He hadn't turned on the light and it was dark in the bathroom. The only light came from the crack under the door. The silky softness of her hair tickled the underside of his chin. Her soft, hiccupy breaths warmed a spot right below his collarbone. One of her arms was looped loosely around his waist. The other was bent with her hand resting on the swell of one of his pecs. He wondered if she could feel the thundering of his heart.

He had questioned his feelings for her on a daily basis. How could he completely fall for a woman he hadn't even kissed? But there was no question now. He had a wad of emotion in his throat the size of a softball. If he could take her pain, he would have. But all he could do was hold her and gently caress her back. He didn't know how long they stood there in the dark. For him, it was not nearly long enough before she drew away.

"I'm sorry," she said in a tear-clogged voice. "I didn't mean to fall apart."

"You didn't fall apart. You just needed to get out all those emotions swirling around inside you. I've cried plenty of times when my emotions got a little too big to handle."

"I find that hard to believe," she said. "I can't see you ever falling apart."

He hadn't removed his hands from her waist and she hadn't removed her hand from his chest. Her fingertips rested along the open edge of his shirt, branding his bare skin like a branding iron left too long in the fire. He tried to stay focused on the conversation and not the feel of her fingertips on his skin and her trim waist beneath his hands.

"I have too. I sobbed just like Ralphie in *A Christmas Story* after I got in a fight with the neighborhood bully—of course, I was the one who got the hell beat out of me. Then I cried again when my high school girlfriend broke up with me. Wept like a baby."

"You had a steady girlfriend?"

"You sound surprised. Do you think I'm too ugly to have a girlfriend?"

Her hand moved, her fingertips caressing bare skin. At least it had felt like a caress. But it had to be an accident. She probably didn't even realize her hand was still there. But he did. Every fiber of his being was focused on her hand and the heat the subtle brush shot through his body.

"Actually," she said. "I thought just the opposite. I thought hot rodeo cowboys had a buckle bunny in every city."

That got his attention. "Hot?"

"Now, who's sounding surprised. I'm sure you know you're hot."

A lot of women had called him hot, but not one time had it made him feel like he wanted to jump up and punch the air. There it was again. Hope. Was it his imagination or had she stepped closer? When he finally spoke, his voice gave away his desire. It was breathless and much lower.

"I didn't have a girl in every city."

"You didn't?"

"No, I didn't. I'm not good at playing the entire dating game. I'm a little too honest about my feelings."

Her fingers moved again, but this time, it wasn't just an accident. She caressed him, her fingertips tracing down the edge of the opening in his shirt. Heat exploded inside of him and parts he didn't want waking up, started waking up.

"There's nothing wrong with being honest about your feelings," she said in a soft, sexy voice that made him even harder. "I have the opposite problem. I've never been honest about my feelings . . . especially with myself. I was so busy trying to be what other people wanted me to be that I pushed down all my feelings."

"I think you let some out today."

There was a smile in her voice when she spoke. "As much as I shouldn't have done it in front of Henry, it *was* liberating. It made me realize that the only thing keeping me trapped in my marriage was my own fear. Once I faced that fear, it stopped having power over me. And my fear wasn't just of Jonathan." Her finger kept stroking and Hayden kept burning. "I tried to convince myself that I stayed with him for so long because I loved him. But really I was just scared of leaving him and having to start a new life. You said it took courage to leave, but if I had left sooner, maybe my son wouldn't have had to go through what he did today."

"You did what you needed to do, Paisley. That's all Henry saw. He saw his mama doing what needed to be done to protect him. You were like this raging mama tiger. And I tell you what. I don't think Jonathan will be messing with you again. You gave him what he deserved and you shouldn't be ashamed of that. You should be proud of it. I sure am."

Her fingers stopped moving. They pressed into his skin for a long moment before they curled and fisted the material of his shirt. Then she did something that completely blindsided him.

She tugged him to her waiting lips.

Hayden was so stunned it took him a second to respond. Paisley was kissing him. And not just kissing him, but devouring him. This was no gentle press of lips. This was a hard, wet kiss with a wicked sweep of tongue that had Hayden's knees buckling. He was used to hesitant, cautious Paisley. He was not used to this aggressive wildcat with the tight grip on his shirt. Her other hand slid into his hair and her fingernails raked along his scalp before she fisted his hair so tightly his eyes watered.

But it wasn't a bad pain. It was a good pain.

With a moan, he pushed her back against the door of the bathroom and took what he'd been wanting for too long. Her sweet lips. Her warm, wet mouth. Her sweeping tongue. He took everything she offered as he pressed his growing erection into her soft, yielding body. She answered his moan with a deep, sexy moan of her own as she hooked a leg around his hips and rubbed her sweet spot against him. He knew where this was going and he wanted to go there. He wanted to go there badly.

Unfortunately, his damn conscience wouldn't let him.

He drew back from the kiss and sighed. "We can't do this, Pea."

She jerked open the snaps of his shirt as she kissed her way down his throat with fiery flicks of her tongue that drove him wild. "Yes, we can. We'll be quiet."

He squeezed his eyes shut and mentally cussed out his conscience. "It's not about being quiet."

She drew back. He missed her sweet lips instantly. "What's it about?"

"You've had an emotional day, Paisley. Having sex with me is another way to get rid of all that energy humming through your veins. And while I'd love to give you that emotional release, I think you'd regret it in the morning. When we make love for the first time, I don't want you regretting anything. Not one damn thing."

Even though he couldn't see her, he could feel the wild, untamed woman fading and the stiff, controlled woman replacing her. He hated that he was responsible. But he also knew he was right. This wasn't the time or the place to show her how much he loved her.

When her leg slipped off his hip and she let go of his shirt, he stepped back and cleared his throat. "Are you going to be okay? You want me to call Everly?"

"No. I'll be fine." Her voice was as cold as ice. As were her eyes when she pulled open the door and sunlight illuminated her face. It was puffy from her tears and her eye was swollen. And yet, she was still the most beautiful woman he had ever seen in his life. He wanted to say something that would make her understand why he had stopped things, but she didn't look like she was in the mood to listen.

So he left.

But damn if it wasn't the hardest thing he'd ever done.

CHAPTER THIRTEEN

"YOU DID WHAT?" Everly stared at Paisley as if she had grown horns.

Maybe Paisley had. She certainly felt different. Like her old skin had peeled off, exposing a new creature that felt a little awkward and unsure . . . but at the same time strong. As strong as a long-horned bull.

She had faced Jonathan and won.

Now here she sat cross-legged on the bed in the Kingmans' guest room sharing something with her sister that was completely out of character for the old Paisley.

"I kissed Hayden."

"Our Hayden?"

Paisley nodded.

Everly's eyes widened before they narrowed. "Wait a second. Are we talking a peck on the cheek to thank him for riding to your rescue—not that it sounded like you needed rescuing." A smile lit her face. "I wish I could've been there to see you pummel that bastard."

"It's not something to be proud of, Ev."

"Hell, yeah, it is. He deserved everything you

gave him. But I don't care about Jonathan. The guy could fall off the face of the earth tomorrow and I wouldn't even make the effort to wave bye-bye. But what I do care about is why my conservative, controlled big sister kissed a man she acted like she hated."

"I don't hate Hayden."

"You didn't like him."

"That was before I got to know him."

Everly waggled her eyebrows. "And it seems like you've gotten to know him well."

"It was just a kiss," she said. Everly didn't let her get away with the lie.

"Liar, liar, pants on fire."

Paisley sighed. "Fine. It was a little more than a kiss."

Everly stared at her. "You had sex with Hayden?"

"Of course not." She hesitated for a second before she told the truth. "But I wanted to. And that's something else I'm not proud of. Kissing Hayden was stupid and crazy and I don't know what got into me. One second, he was praising me for being a tiger mama, and the next second, I was kissing him. And not just kissing him, but climbing his body like a maypole." She blushed just thinking about how sexually aggressive she'd been.

"Hey, that's not crazy. I'm sure there are a lot of women who would love to climb Hayden like a maypole. He's a good guy who knows how to treat a woman. After Jonathan, he's just the man you need."

"I don't need a man."

"If you mauled Hayden, I'd say you do. So what stopped you from having sex with him?"

She flopped back on the pillows as she relived her humiliation. "He did. He said I had been through too much emotional trauma and he didn't want me doing something I'd regret in the morning."

Everly lay down next to her and sighed. "Okay, I think Hayden might have just won the Sweetest Guy This Side of the Mississippi award. If I didn't love him before, I'd love him now." She turned her head and looked at Paisley. "And since you're beating yourself up for kissing him, I figure he was right. You would've regretted it."

"Of course I would have. I shouldn't have even kissed him. Now he'll think I'm hot for his body."

Everly studied her. "Are you?"

That was a good question. One Paisley didn't have an answer for. Or maybe she had an answer, but just wasn't willing to accept it. Especially when she wasn't about to do anything about it.

"I'm not getting involved with another man. Jonathan tangled my emotions so much that it's going to take years to untangle them. Until then, it would be stupid to get into another relation-ship."

"I'm not talking about getting into another relationship," Everly said. "I'm talking about sex. Plain ol' down-and-dirty sex. People have it all the time, Paise, and it doesn't have to turn into a lifelong commitment."

Just the thought of having down-and-dirty sex with Hayden made Paisley's body heat up like a curling iron set on high. Obviously, she *was* hot for his body. And if the erection he'd pressed against her was any indication, he was hot for hers too. What had he said? *When we make love for the first time, I don't want you regretting anything.* Not if they made love, but when.

She shook her head. "No. No sex. Down-and-dirty or otherwise. I need to focus on making a new life for me and Henry."

Her lawyer had called her that morning to tell her Jonathan had signed the divorce papers—this time in front of his lawyers. He hadn't contested anything and had given her complete custody of Henry, along with child support and a hefty settlement. Part of her wanted to punch the air and crow like a rooster. But there was still a part of her that was scared. Henry had been through so much. What if she couldn't give him everything she wanted to give him?

Everly read her thoughts. "You will make a new life for you and Henry, Paise. I just hope it's right here in Cursed."

She hoped so too. She had come to love the little town with its kindhearted people and couldn't see her and Henry living anywhere else. But there were other things to consider than just her desires. "I guess it will depend on where I can find a job once I get my nursing certificate."

Everly stared at her. "You're going to become a nurse?" She pulled Paisley into her arms and hugged her tight. "Oh, Paise, that's awesome. It's what you've always wanted." She drew back, and there were tears in her eyes. "I'm so happy for you . . . even if it takes you away from me."

Paisley cupped her face in her hands. "You're my baby sister. I'm not ever going to let anything, or anyone, take me away from you again. I'm not planning on leaving the state, which means, even if I do have to move to a bigger city, we can still see each other often."

"It won't be as nice as getting to see you every day." Everly sent her a wobbly smile. "I've gotten pretty attached to my big sister. And my chatterbox nephew. Where is Henry, anyway?"

"Stetson took him out to the stables this morning after breakfast. He's still upset about what happened yesterday. I tried to talk to him about it, but he ignored me. I guess he'll talk about it when he's ready."

"Of course he will. That kid doesn't keep anything in. He just needs some time to process it." She sent Paisley a pointed look. "And so do you."

"I've been processing things since leaving Jonathan. I have finally come to realize that there was nothing I could've done to fix my marriage. Or Jonathan. Now I'm just ready to put everything behind me and move on."

"Are you going to move back in with Hester? You know you're always welcome at the parsonage."

"I know, but I think Hester has missed us." She grinned. "Besides, I wouldn't want Henry and me putting a kink in your and Chance's newlywed fun. But for the time being, I think we're going to stay at the ranch. The Kingmans have assured me we're more than welcome and I think the ranch is just what Henry needs to get over the trauma he's experienced. But I'll still come into town and help you at the bar."

Everly shook her head. "You're not coming back to work at Nasty Jack's. If you're going to get your nursing license, you'll need to study. And you can't study if you're working every night at a bar."

"I'll study during the day."

"And take care of Henry? After what he's been through, he needs his mama more than ever. No, you need to focus on your son and becoming a nurse. With the settlement Jonathan gave you, you don't have to worry about money." Everly smiled. "Obviously, all the man needed was a little cowboy persuasion to do what was right."

Paisley stared at her. "A little cowboy persuasion?"

Everly looked away. "Did I say cowboy? I meant tough sister persuasion." She got up from the bed. "Now, let's go see what my nephew is up to. If he's anything like his aunt, it will be no good."

When they got to the stables, they found Henry perched on the railing of the corral with Stetson standing next to him. Little Teddy was strapped to Stetson's chest in a baby carrier. Paisley barely had time to "aww" over the cute sight of the tough ranch owner with his tiny son before her gaze got caught by the handsome cowboy astride the big horse. She hadn't seen Hayden since their kiss and she had the sudden urge to turn tail and run back to the house. She might have done so if Hayden's gaze hadn't landed on her and frozen her in her tracks.

She had convinced herself that he was right—that her uncharacteristic behavior the day before had to do with a need to release all the emotions from her encounter with Jonathan. But that theory was blown to hell as soon as Hayden's cobalt eyes touched her. Like a bolt of lightning, a shaft of desire shot straight through her, leaving her feeling shaky, flushed, and breathless—along with humiliated by her brazen behavior.

But Hayden didn't show any signs of remembering what had happened between them. He didn't flash her a knowing smile or a wink. He merely tipped his hat and returned his attention to the horse.

It was the same stallion that had given the ranch hands all the trouble the other day. At least it looked like Spunky. It certainly didn't act like him. Gone was the animal with wild eyes and a bad attitude. In its place was a well-mannered horse that seemed to be showing off. He pranced in a pretty trot around the corral like a show pony before he started doing other tricks: walking backward and turning in quick circles, first one way and then the other.

When she and Everly stepped up to the railing, Paisley couldn't help asking Stetson about the horse. "That's not Spunky, is it?"

Henry answered for him. "Yeah, it is, Mama! That's Spunky! Isn't he great?"

"But he acted so wild the other day."

Stetson spoke. "Sometimes all a horse needs is

to feel secure. Once Hayden made Spunky realize no one was going to harm him, the horse's
true colors came out. Of course, it helps that
Hayden knows horses. Watch the way he gives
Spunky directions with just the shift of his body
or pressure of his legs."

Paisley stared at Hayden. "Hayden is the one
telling the horse what to do?"

"I told you he was a real cowboy, Mama!"
Henry yelled with excitement. He waved his
hand over his head. "Hey, Hay! Show Mama how
you can get Spunky to dance."

Once again, Hayden's gaze landed on Paisley.
Once again, she felt like she had been tossed into
a dryer that had been set on high heat. He held
her gaze as the horse started hopping from one
front hoof to the other. She was impressed. And
not just with the horse.

Hayden sat a saddle well. Under his light western shirt and faded jeans, his muscles flexed and
released as he guided the horse without using the
reins. He would probably make love the same
way—guiding his partner with gentle ease to a
mind-blowing climax.

She blinked. What was she thinking? Especially
with her son standing so close.

"Hmm? Are you sure you're not interested in
down-and-dirty sex?" Everly whispered close
to her ear. "Because if the way you're looking
at that man is any indication, you're interested,
sis. Extremely interested." Before Paisley could
shush her sister, Everly drew away and looked at
Henry. "Hey, cute cowboy, are you gonna notice

your favorite aunt? Or have horses completely replaced me in your heart?"

"Hey, Aunt Eberly! You want to see the cutest horse eber?" He looked down at Stetson from his perch on the fence. "Can we, Stet? Can we show Aunt Eberly Glory Boy?"

"We sure can." Stetson helped him down from the railing. Henry immediately ran over and grabbed Everly's hand and pulled her toward the stables.

"You're gonna lobe Glory, Aunt Eberly!"

Paisley planned to follow everyone into the stables, but she'd only taken a few steps when Hayden stopped her.

"Paisley."

For a second, she wanted to pretend like she hadn't heard him. Then she realized she would have to face him sooner or later. It would be better to get it over with now. Although she couldn't stop her face from heating as he walked the horse to the railing where she stood. The horse looked much bigger up close and she took a step back.

"No need to be afraid of Spunky. He's much calmer now that he realizes I won't hurt him." He hesitated and his gaze grew more intense. "I won't hurt you either, Paisley."

She answered truthfully. "I know that."

He smiled. "Good." He swung down from the horse, then expertly climbed the fence, side-vaulting over the last rung and landing much too close for comfort. "So I guess you're feeling a little embarrassed about last night."

"No," she lied.

His eyebrows lifted beneath the brim of his hat. "Really? Then you must've gotten a sun-burn while you were sleeping because your face is redder than my mama's late August tomatoes." He gently touched the corner of her eye. "How's your eye? It looks a lot less swollen today."

His touch had more than her face filling with heat. She tried to concentrate on his question and not the tingling feeling radiating through her body. "It's a little tender, but I've had worse." His eyes darkened with anger and she quickly changed the subject. "I need to apologize about what happened yesterday."

His eyebrows hiked again. "If you're talking about what happened in the bathroom, you don't have to apologize for giving me the best kiss of my life."

If hearts could do gymnastics, hers felt like it did a double flip with a twist. *The best kiss of his life?*

"And just so you know," he continued. "I've been wanting to kiss you for a long time."

She stared at him dumbstruck. "You have?"

"Yep. But I couldn't very well do it when you were still married and you pretty much hated my guts." He smiled a slow, sexy smile that made everything inside her feel like melting butter. "It's good to know that you don't still hate me."

No, she didn't hate him. What she felt for him wasn't even close to hate. And it scared her. No matter what she felt, she wasn't ready to get back into a relationship. She had to make that perfectly clear. To Hayden. And herself.

"What happened last night can't happen again, Hayden. You were right. It was just an emotional release after everything I'd been through. I want to thank you for stopping it when you did because I'm not ready to get involved with anyone right now. Not when I'm still trying to figure out who I am and what I want."

His smile faded. "I get that. But there's something you need to know." His blue eyes pinned her with an intensity that took her breath away. "When you figure out who you are and what you want, I'll be right here." He placed an arm around her waist and pulled her up to her toes. "Right here."

He kissed her. A slow, deep, thorough kiss that made her completely forget the words she'd just spoken. But before she could even start to kiss him back, he released her and tipped his hat.

"Have a good day, Sweet Pea." He climbed back over the fence and led Spunky into the stables.

CHAPTER FOURTEEN

HAYDEN HAD ALWAYS thought he was a patient man. But it had only been a couple weeks since he had kissed Paisley by the paddock and vowed to wait until she figured things out and he already felt like a man stretched on a torture rack. He spent his nights tossing and turning and replaying his and Paisley's kisses over and over in his head while he spent his days trying to catch a glimpse of her.

It wasn't easy. She spent most of her time in the house, playing with Henry or studying for her nursing test. Everly had told him that if she passed and got state certified, she might be leaving Cursed to take a job elsewhere. Hayden couldn't stand the thought of that.

He knew Paisley was estranged from her parents. So Everly was all the family she and Henry had. Paisley had just reconnected with her sister. They needed each other. And Henry adored his aunt and uncle. And Hester. He had also become attached to everyone on the Kingman Ranch. They had become attached to him. All the cow boys watched out for him and taught him how to swing a lasso and scoop poop and spit. All the Kingmans treated him like he was one of their own.

While Hayden had had a good childhood and loving parents, he still would have loved growing up on a ranch surrounded by a large family. He wanted Henry to have that.

Which posed a problem.

If Paisley did choose him, what was he going to do? He couldn't ask her and Henry to move away from all the people they'd come to love. Their lives had been chaotic enough. He wasn't about to cause more disruption.

But he already had land in Montana. Not to mention that his mama and daddy were there. He missed them. Although he knew when he left Texas, he would miss it too.

He couldn't put a finger on exactly what it was about the country that drew him in. It wasn't nearly as green or lush as Montana. There were no majestic mountains. Very few lakes and streams. The weather was unpredictable. You could be freezing one day and sweltering the next. The wind seemed to blow all the time. Tornados, hail, and drought were just accepted as part of Texas life.

And yet, there was something about sitting on a horse and seeing acres and acres of cattle country spread out before you with no mountains or trees to take away from the endless sky. The soft pinks of a Texas sunrise made a man feel at peace with the world. The flaming oranges of a sunset made that same man feel like he could take on anything.

Then there were the people. Once they sized you up and decided they liked you, you became part of their family.

The Kingmans were a perfect example. They had opened their arms to Hayden and treated him like one of their own. So much so that he felt even guiltier about his deception. And Uncle Jack didn't help matters. The old guy had kept his secret, but every time Hayden ran into him, Uncle Jack's eagle eyes made him feel judged.

Or maybe Hayden was just judging himself.

"Hey, Hay!"

Henry's greeting cut into Hayden's thoughts and he glanced at the door of the stables to see the little boy strut in as if he owned the place. He certainly owned Hayden's heart. Hayden had fallen head over heels in love with Henry just like he had with Paisley. Spending time with Henry made waiting for Paisley to figure things out a little easier . . . and a whole lot harder. If Paisley decided she wasn't interested in Hayden, he'd have two cracks in his heart. But the fact that Paisley had started to let Henry come down to the stables and spend time with him had to be a good sign.

"Hey, partner," Hayden said. "I was just going to bring Glory Boy in from the paddock, you want to help me groom him?"

"Yes, sir!"

Glory seemed as happy to see Henry as Henry

was to see the colt. He followed Henry into his stall without Hayden having to coax him with a treat. Then he stood still while Hayden taught Henry how to use a currycomb.

"Can Glory Boy be my horse, Hay?" Henry asked as he brushed the colt.

"I'm sorry, partner, but Glory Boy isn't mine to give. He belongs to the Kingmans and they all love him as much as you do."

"Nuh-uh. I lobe him to the moon and back." Henry stopped grooming and looked at Hayden. "I lobe you to the moon and back too, Hay."

The lump that formed in Hayden's throat was hard to talk around. "I love you too, partner."

A crease formed along Henry's forehead. "I don't think my daddy lobes me."

The lump in Hayden's throat grew. Jonathan hadn't abused Henry physically, but his lack of attention had abused him mentally. Hayden knew exactly how that felt. "I know how you feel, partner. My daddy didn't love me either."

Henry's eyes widened. "But you said that your daddy was a good daddy. You said he taught you how to ride a horse and how to build a birdhouse and how to 'spect women."

"Jimmy is my stepdaddy."

"What's a stepdaddy?"

Hayden tried to come up with an explanation Henry would understand. "Sometimes mamas and daddies don't stay together. Like your mama, my mama left my daddy."

"Was your daddy mean to your mama?"

"I don't know that I'd say he was mean, but he didn't love her. From what I've learned about him, I don't think he could love anyone."

"Was he a cowboy like you?"

"Yes, but I don't think he wanted to be. I think his daddy forced him to be and that made him unhappy. Sometimes when you're unhappy, you take it out on people you shouldn't."

"Like mamas."

"Yes, like mamas . . . and kids. But lucky for me, my mama found a new daddy for me. My stepdaddy had no problem loving my mama or loving me."

Henry's eyes crinkled in thought for a moment before he spoke. "Can you be my stepdaddy, Hay?"

Hayden blinked back the tears that came to his eyes. "Well, partner, I'd like nothing better. But there are a lot of things that go into becoming a stepdaddy. Those things need to be decided by adults."

"Like you and Mama."

"Yes. Like me and your mama." He took the currycomb from him. "Now you better get on up to the house. Potts should have lunch ready about now." He held opened the stall door.

Henry rushed over and gave Hayden's legs a tight hug that made Hayden's heart swell once again to his throat before he hurried out the door. "Hey, Stet! Guess what? I got to comb Glory's hair and he looks as good as new."

Hayden stepped out of the stall expecting to find Stetson grinning at Henry's comment.

Instead, he had a funny look on his face. "Something wrong, Stet?" Hayden asked.

Stetson studied him for a long moment before he shook his head. "No. Nothing's wrong. I just came to talk to you about a project I wanted your help with."

Hayden thought the project would be something to do with the ranch. So he was surprised when he stepped into Stetson's office and Stet pulled out plans for a tree house.

"I know it seems a little over the top for a tree house," Stetson said. "But my granddaddy had it built for me and my siblings and we spent a lot of time there as kids. When it was swept away in a tornado, we were all pretty upset. I thought it would be nice to rebuild it exactly the way it was for our kids." He glanced at Hayden. "Heritage is important. It helps us remember where we came from. And since your . . . stepdaddy was a carpenter, I figure you'd be the right one to help with the project."

Hayden studied the plans. He remembered the tree house. Mystic and Buck had been in it when the tornado hit and Hayden had warned them and helped them get to safety. It might have been as lavish and pretentious as the castle with its glass windows and balcony, but it was also cool as hell. He could understand why Stetson wanted to rebuild it. He wanted his children and nieces and nephews to create their own memories in a tree house their great-grandfather had designed.

"I'll be happy to help, but it will take some time."

"Not if all of us chip in."

The next day, the Kingman brothers, Gage, Shane, and even Chance, met Hayden at the huge oak that had once held the tree house. After they unloaded the wood and tools, they got to work. Hayden soon realized the Kingmans weren't as proficient with a hammer and saw as they were with a rope and horse.

And it didn't help that Wolfe and Buck loved to fight and argue.

"You just knocked my hammer off the ledge, you clumsy idiot," Wolfe growled.

"I did not. You knocked it off," Buck said. "I can't help it if you have feet the size of rowboats."

"It's better than having a big mouth that doesn't know when to shut up."

There was a scuffling sound and Hayden glanced up at the platform high in the oak tree to see Wolfe and Buck wrestling. Since there were only two walls attached to the platform, Hayden was worried one, or both, of the Kingmans were going to tumble over the side.

"That's enough!" he yelled up.

Both Wolfe and Buck stopped and looked down. Even Gage, Shane, Chance, and Stetson stopped what they were doing and looked at Hayden. Since he was only an employee, he shouldn't have said anything. But Stetson had asked him to spearhead the project and he wasn't going to be responsible for someone busting open his head.

"You want to wrestle?" he said. "Do it on the ground where you won't fall and kill yourselves."

Buck gave Wolfe a sock in the arm before he

went back to work. But Wolfe stood there staring at Hayden. Hayden figured he was about to get a piece of Wolfe's temper. Instead, he got a smile.

"Toss up my hammer, would you, Hay?"

The ranchers and preacher might not be carpenters, but they were dedicated hard workers. If they made a mistake, they stuck with it until they got it right. By late afternoon, the tree house had walls, a shingled room, new windows, and a staircase encircling the thick trunk of the tree.

There was a feeling of pride and camaraderie when all seven men stood back and looked at their accomplishment. The wood needed to be stained and shutters put on the windows. But all and all, it looked just like the old tree house King had built. Hayden couldn't help wondering if his grandfather was looking down with pride.

He hoped so.

"We did it!" Buck hooked an arm over Wolfe's shoulder. "Now all it needs is a king-sized mattress and a few candles." When everyone looked at him, he shrugged. "I figure we might as well use it as a love nest until our kids are old enough to enjoy it."

Wolfe snorted. "Love nest? Just wait until your baby girl arrives, little brother. You won't be thinking about using it as a love nest as much as a place to take a nap. I swear I haven't had a full night's sleep since Maribelle got here."

"Me either." Gage held up a hand. "I'll buy the napping mattress if I can have first dibs."

Buck glanced over to Hayden. "If anyone should get first dibs, it's Hay. Without his help, it would've looked like a dilapidated shed in a tree." His eyes twinkled. "And I'm sure he's not going to want to use it for napping." He spoke in an annoying singsong voice. "Paisley and Hayden sittin' in a tree." When Hayden showed surprise, he laughed. "Anyone with eyes could've figured it out, Hay. Whenever she's around, you can't focus on anything. The other day, you were so busy mooning over her that you stepped in a big pile of horseshit."

Hayden scowled. "Every cowboy steps in horseshit from time to time."

"But you didn't even know you did it. You just stood there in that stinky, steaming pile staring at Paisley as if she was a queen who had just graced you with her presence."

Damn. He didn't even remember stepping in horse poop. All he remembered was how beautiful Paisley had looked in her skinny jeans and white T-shirt. For the first time, she'd had on a pair of cowboy boots. Since they hadn't been new, he figured she'd borrowed them from one of the Kingman women. Those boots had pulled up all kinds of images. Sweet ones of them riding horses together and naughty ones of her wrapping those boots around his waist as he sank deep inside her.

When he snapped out of his daydream, he realized all six men were looking at him with knowing smiles.

He sighed and run a hand through his hair. "Okay, so I'm in love with Paisley."

"Does she know how you feel?" Chance asked.

"No, and telling her will only make her feel like I'm putting her in a corner and forcing her into something she's not ready for."

Wolfe spoke. "But what if she's ready and she's just scared to take another chance. It makes sense given the man she was married to." He grinned. "I thoroughly enjoyed making that asshole squirm."

"Squirm?" Hayden looked at Stetson. "I thought you were going to let the sheriff handle Jonathan."

Stetson shrugged. "I did . . . after I had a little talk with him and mentioned that there had been numerous people who had gone missing when they made the mistake of trespassing on Kingman land. On thousands of acres, it was real easy to bury a body so it would never be found."

Buck laughed. "Jonathan looked like he was about to piss his pants. Especially when Wolfe pulled out his gun."

"I was just checking to see if it needed cleaning," Wolfe said, innocently. "But we've gotten off the topic." He looked at Hayden. "If you love Paisley, I think you should tell her. Take it from me, keeping your feelings a secret never works out."

The rest of the men nodded in agreement.

Everyone but Stetson.

"This isn't just about telling her that you love her. Love is one thing. A commitment is another. Not just to her, but to her son. Are you ready to make that commitment, Hayden? Even if it completely changes all the plans you had for your future?"

As Hayden stood there with his feet firmly planted on Kingman land, staring at the men who were not only blood, but also his friends, he knew the answer.

CHAPTER FIFTEEN

"AND YOU KNOW what else, Mama? Hay has big muscles. Like really big muscles. The other day, we took off our shirts so we could wash off our sweating with the hose. And Hay has big boobs. But they aren't soft like yours. They're hard."

Paisley squeezed her eyes shut to block out the image of Hayden's hard boobs covered with droplets of water. The last couple weeks, she had been struggling to keep her mind off Hayden and now it seemed he was all her son could talk about. Since coming back from the stables yesterday, Henry had been filling her ears with all of Hayden's attributes.

"And you know what else? He can make them jump. I bet if I asked him, he'd show you."

"No!" Her loud response caused Henry to rear back in the desk chair he was sitting in. She softened her voice. "Thank you, but I don't want to see Hayden's . . . muscles jump. Now finish writing your name so you can get washed up before we go down to dinner."

Henry went back to writing his first and last

name on the homework sheet his preschool teacher had given him while Paisley tried to go back to reading the nursing textbook. But her mind kept returning to jumping muscles.

She couldn't blame Henry. Her mind seemed to always go back to Hayden. It wasn't so bad during the day when she was busy, but at night all she could think about was Hayden lying in his bed . . . completely naked. Then she'd start thinking about what would happen if she had the courage to slip down the stairs and claim what she wanted.

And she wanted Hayden. There was no more denying it. The only thing keeping her from taking what she wanted was fear. Fear of getting involved with a man who would end up hurting her.

But with each passing day, her fear was lessening. Hayden West was a kind and caring man. He was kind and caring with horses and the other animals. He was kind and caring to the Kingmans and all the ranch hands. And he was kind and caring with Henry. Everyone seemed to love and trust him.

Why couldn't she?

It wasn't like Hayden hadn't proven his trustworthiness time and time again. So why was she hesitating? Why was she letting fear keep her from going after what she wanted?

She glanced at her son who was diligently writing his name with his tongue sticking out the side of his mouth.

Henry.

She wasn't just scared about Hayden hurting her. She was scared about him hurting Henry. She would never forgive herself if she allowed her son to get hurt by another man. He had enough wounds from Jonathan. Wounds he would carry with him for the rest of his life. She refused to add to them by making another bad choice.

She pulled him close. "I love you, Henry James."

"I lobe you too, Mama, but you made me mess up my S and now it really looks like a snake."

She laughed as she kissed the top of his head. "You can fix it later. For now, let's get washed up for dinner."

She and Henry arrived in the kitchen before the Kingmans. Being that it was Potts's date night with Kitty Carson, he had set up dinner buffet style. Casserole dishes on hot plates lined the large island and a big basket of steaming dinner rolls sat in the center of the long harvest table.

"Go ahead and help yourselves," Potts said as he took off his apron. "I'm already late and if any woman doesn't like to be kept waitin', it's Kitty." He ruffled Henry's hair as he walked by. "I made you cowboy cookies, but you can't have one until after you eat your supper."

Henry beamed. "Thanks, Potts."

Once Potts was gone and Paisley started filling Henry's plate, the Kingmans started showing up. Lily with Teddy arrived first, then Adeline with Danny, Gretchen with Maribelle, Mystic, and finally Delaney. Mystic barely had a baby bump, but Delaney's stomach stuck out in front of her like the bow of a ship. As Paisley watched her ease down into a chair, she couldn't help feeling sorry for her. Her doctor had given her strict orders to stay away from any ranch work and rest. For Delaney, that was like being in hell.

"I swear," she grumbled as she rubbed her large belly. "If these two don't get out soon, I'm going to go crazy."

"They'll be here soon enough," Mystic said. "Your due date is only a week away."

"A week might not seem that long to some people, but to a woman who has to run to the bathroom every two seconds, can't see her feet, and can't step foot out the door without her brothers and husband hovering over her like she's a fragile piece of glass, it's a lifetime. And I'm over it!"

Henry sat down at the table with his plate. "How are those babies gonna get out of your tummy, Del?"

"That's a good question, sport. Believe me, I'm wondering the same thing. Because it doesn't seem possible to squeeze two babies out of such a tiny—"

Paisley cut her off before she could go into too much detail. "Here, let me cut your asparagus, Henry."

As she was cutting his asparagus, the sound of clicking boots on tile floors had her turning to the doorway that led to the mudroom. A second later, six cowboys stepped into the kitchen.

But only one held Paisley's attention.

Hayden's T-shirt fit him as snug as always and Paisley couldn't keep her gaze from lowering to his chest and the swell of his hard pectoral muscles. The memory of him sitting in bed naked flashed through her head, igniting a flood of desire that made her feel flushed and breathless. When she lifted her gaze and was caught in the cobalt blue of his eyes, the feeling only intensified.

Thankfully, Henry averted her attention when he started bouncing up and down in his chair.

"Hay! Hay! Are you gonna eat dinner with us?"

"If that's okay with everyone."

It wasn't okay. How could she get through the meal when Hayden stood there looking more delectable than the food Potts had prepared?

"Yay!" Henry squealed. "Sit next to Mama, Hay. She'll cut your 'paragus for you."

Buck greeted Mystic with a kiss before he gave Hayden a teasing grin. "Yeah, Hay. Fill up a plate and sit right down there next to Henry's mama and let her cut your asparagus."

Hayden's gaze narrowed on Buck, which had the youngest Kingman laughing and slapping him hard on the back. The other men seemed to find it amusing too. They all shot Hayden a grin as they headed to the counter to get their food.

She had noticed before how easily Hayden fit in with the Kingmans. What she hadn't noticed was how much he resembled them. Especially Stetson. They were both big men with broad shoulders and thick muscles. They both had dark brown hair, deep-set eyes, and strong jawlines. She would have continued to study their similarities if Hayden hadn't moved around the counter, presenting her with his butt in his worn Wrangler jeans.

He had one fine butt.

Suddenly, she had the strong urge to reach out and slip her hand inside the stitched pocket and feel the firm curved muscle flex against her palm.

She jerked her gaze away and mentally chastised herself. *Get a grip, Paisley!*

But it was impossible to get a grip when he sat down in the chair next to her. Heat seemed to emanate from him like a space heater. It was comforting and soothing and, at the same time, made her feel like a drop of water on a sizzling hot griddle—jumpy and ready to dissolve into Hayden's heat.

"Hi, Paisley." The low timbre of his voice almost melted her panties.

She swallowed hard and tried to keep her voice steady. "Hey."

He leaned closer and his breath ruffled the hair by her ear. "I like it when you call me Hay."

She squeezed her eyes closed and prayed she could make it through dinner without doing something really stupid . . . like diving on Hayden and getting rid of all her sexual frustrations.

Thankfully, he didn't try to talk to her again. The Kingmans kept him in conversation by asking about his life in Montana. Paisley couldn't even listen. She was too busy keeping her rioting libido in check. When he reached for a dinner roll and accidentally brushed her arm with his, she almost jumped out of her chair.

It was more than a little annoying that he could

sit there talking and laughing with all the King-mans while she struggled to keep from melting at his boots. She was relieved when the meal was over. Since everyone had babies or was pregnant, she volunteered to do the dishes. Hayden stood and started helping her stack the plates, but the last thing she needed was him staying to help her do dishes.

"I got it," she said a little more harshly than she intended.

His blue eyes reflected hurt before he nodded. "Okay." He ruffled Henry's hair. "Night, partner."

"Night, Hay." Henry wrapped his arms around Hayden's legs and gave him a tight hug.

Once everyone was gone, Paisley quickly rinsed and loaded all the glasses, silverware, and plates into the dishwasher, then left the casserole dishes to soak in soapy water while she took Henry upstairs and got him ready for bed.

After she read him a story and tucked him in, he looked up at her with hazel eyes that were so much like Everly's. "Do you like Hay, Mama?"

"Of course I like him." A little more than she wanted to.

"Then why didn't you talk to him at dinner? And how come you wouldn't let him help you with the dishes? I think Hay likes to help you."

Since she wasn't about to explain her com-plicated emotions to a five-year-old, she only nodded. "You're right. I shouldn't be so mean to Hay."

After Henry fell asleep, Paisley headed back downstairs to finish the dishes. It looked like the Kingmans had gone to bed too. The house was dark except for the light coming from the kitchen. She wondered how they had known she was coming back down. She got her answer when she stepped into the kitchen and saw Hayden standing at the sink rinsing a pan.

She didn't know if he heard her or just sensed her, but before she could make her escape, he turned.

Once again, his gaze snagged hers. In those blue depths she saw the same hunger she'd been feeling all night. He set the pan down and whispered one word.

"Pea."

The nickname had sounded so cute spoken in Everly's high, babyish voice. In Hayden's deep, husky one it sounded anything but cute. It sounded like a reverent prayer. Like a desperate plea. Like a devout promise . . . of all things naughty and wonderful.

It settled in the emptiest part of Paisley and planted itself. For once, she didn't feel like an imperfect daughter. An abused wife. A failed mother. She felt like . . . a desirable woman.

Any fear she still had completely evaporated and she moved toward him. He met her halfway. She gripped his shirt and tugged him closer while his hands wrapped around her waist and completely lifted her off her feet.

Their mouths met like two rockets colliding. Explosive and hot. There was no finesse. No gentle glide of tongues and lips. There was just savage need. Paisley held nothing back from him and

Hayden held nothing back from her. Amid deep moans and needy groans, they tasted and licked and nipped while their hands ran over each other's bodies in a frenzied search for bare skin.

Paisley found it first when she tugged the snaps of Hayden's western shirt open and ran her hands over the hard muscles beneath. When she cupped his pec, it jumped beneath her palm. She flicked his nipple with her thumbnail and loved the low growl it caused him to make. His hands slid down to her butt and he gripped each cheek tightly as he rubbed his hard erection against her. Heat pooled inside her and she whimpered with need.

He drew back from her lips and trailed kisses down her throat as his grip tightened on her butt. "I got you, baby. I got you."

"I need . . . I need . . ."

He bit a spot on her neck just below her ear before licking it better. "I know what you need and I'm going to give it to you. I'm going to give it to you all night long." He released her butt and picked her up, carrying her into his bedroom off the kitchen. Once he'd closed the door, he set her back on her feet, stripped off his shirt, and pushed her against the door with a slide of hungry lips and the firm press of his body.

He wasn't gentle. His grip on her butt cheeks was tight, the grind of his body hard, the nip of his teeth on her neck slightly painful. He wanted her with an intensity that should have terrified her. Instead, it made her feel desired, needed . . . empowered. Deep down, she knew any time she wanted him to stop, all she had to do was say so and he would.

But the only sound she made were moans and whimpers as he stripped her naked and urged her body to experience feelings it had never experienced before. She understood how Spunky had felt. Hayden made her want to follow his every lead. He led her down a path of pure pleasure with the tug of his lips on her nipples and the stroke of his fingers on her skin.

When she thought she couldn't take another second of his delicious torture, he knelt at her feet and kissed her like she had never been kissed before. His greedy mouth settled on the quivering spot between her legs and took her to a new level of desire. A level where she lost all thought of the past and the future and just focused on the moment and reaching the mind-blowing climax his sipping lips and flicking tongue promised.

Her orgasm came in a rush of feelings so intense that she fisted his hair and cried out as she rode the waves that consumed her. He held her to his mouth until her knees gave out and she slipped to the floor in front of him.

Once she came back to reality, awkwardness set in. She was glad for the darkness of the room. Still, she felt like she should say something.

"Thank you."

There was laughter in his reply. "Thank you."

"But you didn't . . ."

He found her hand and linked their fingers. They had just experienced an extremely intimate act, and yet, for some reason, sitting there in the dark holding hands seemed even more intimate. "Just because I didn't reach orgasm doesn't mean I didn't thoroughly enjoy giving you one." He hesitated. "Not to say that I wouldn't mind having one."

All awkwardness disappeared and she laughed. "Here on the floor?"

His thumb brushed back and forth over her hand. "Tempting, but I'm thinkin' that big ol' bed only a couple feet away might be more comfortable." He stood and pulled her to her feet. "I just need to move my duffel." He gave her a long, sensual kiss before he released her and stepped away.

A second later, a lamp came on and Paisley scooped up her shirt and held it in front of her so she wouldn't be standing there completely naked while Hayden picked up the stack of shirts and underwear sitting on the bed and shoved them into his half-full duffel before moving it off the bed.

When he turned back to her, he frowned. "I don't ever want you to feel shy with me, Pea. If you want, I can turn the light back off. But I just want you to know I've dreamed about this moment for a long time and I would love to have that dream come true."

She hesitated for only a moment before she lowered the shirt and let it drop to the floor.

She had never been overly proud of her body. Everly was the one with full breasts and shapely hips. Paisley had little of either. As Hayden's gaze ran over her, she figured he would be sadly disappointed.

He wasn't.

When his gaze lifted, his eyes held awe. "Damn. You're more beautiful than I ever imagined." He walked over to her and cradled her face in his palm. "And tonight, you're mine." He kissed her.

This kiss was much slower and gentler than the others . . . as were his caresses as he guided her down to the bed. While she watched, he finished undressing. She was thankful she hadn't had him turn off the light. Clothed, he was hot. Nude, he was magnificent. She wished she was an artist so she could capture his beauty.

When he was completely naked, he got a condom from his wallet before he joined her on the bed. Amid soft kisses, he aligned himself with her. The fit was snug, but perfect. Their bodies seemed to recognize each other immediately. Like an old married couple that had danced to the same song all their lives. He could sense when she wanted him to move deeper and faster and she knew exactly when to meet each thrust. She had always had a problem reaching orgasm during sex with Jonathan. She had no such problem with Hayden. It came out of nowhere, lifting her and holding her suspended in a maelstrom of sensations.

It wasn't as physically intense as the previous one, but it was twice as emotionally intense. While the waves of pleasure crashed over her, Hayden never looked away from her. She remained locked in the midnight blue of his eyes from the moment her orgasm hit to the last thrust and shiver of his.

Once they were spent, he spooned around her and cradled her tightly in his arms as if he didn't ever want to let her go.

But right before she nodded off, something struck her.

Something she hadn't given any thought to until now.

"Why were you packing?"

CHAPTER SIXTEEN

HAYDEN WAS IN heaven. Paisley was in his arms. And she didn't act like she was in any hurry to leave. He didn't want her to leave.

Ever.

He tightened his arms and sighed with contentment as he answered her question. "I'm leaving for Montana first thing in the morning."

He didn't want to go—especially after what had happened tonight—but after talking with Shane, Chance, and his half-brothers, he'd realized Texas was where he wanted to make his home. He planned to head back to Montana and take care of all his loose ends before he came back here and fully committed to winning Paisley's heart. Tonight had proven he had a chance of doing that. He knew she wasn't ready to jump back into love, but she wasn't the kind of woman who took sex lightly either. She wouldn't go to bed with a man she didn't care about and trust.

Now all he needed to do was tell his mama and daddy, sell his land, take all his stuff out of storage, and—

His mental list of things he needed to do was

cut off when Paisley pulled away from him and got out of bed. Even though he knew she needed to get back to Henry, he couldn't help wanting her to stay a little longer.

"Do you need to go so soon?"

She didn't answer as she pulled on her shirt. He missed the sight of her perfect breasts and the constellation of freckles that started at her left shoulder and stretched to the top of her right breast. Once her shirt was on, she grabbed her jeans from the floor and tugged them on, offering him the briefest glimpse of sweet ass before it was covered. There was something about her jerky movements that alerted him something was wrong.

He got out of bed. "Are you mad, Pea?"

"No. I'm not mad." She grabbed her bra and panties and stuffed them into the pockets of her jeans. "I'm not mad at all. Why would I be mad? I'm fine. Just fine." She grabbed her boot, but then froze as if someone had tagged her during a game of freeze tag. Before he could ask her what was wrong, she straightened and the boot came sailing right at his head.

"You, sonofabitch! How could you?"

Hayden barely ducked in time. The boot slammed into the wall as she picked up the other one.

"I thought you were different. I thought you were someone I could count on. But you're just like Jonathan!" She threw the other boot, but Hayden was ready for it this time and caught it. He stared at her in confusion.

"Why are you mad at me? What did I do?"

Paisley's eyes flared with anger. "If you don't know, then you are a jerk. But you're right. I shouldn't be mad at you. I should be mad at myself. I knew better than to trust another man, but what did I do?" She threw up her hands. "I trusted another man. And I didn't just trust him with my emotions. I trusted him with my son's."

Hayden didn't have a clue what was happening. "What does Henry have to do with us having sex?"

"Sex? This doesn't have to do with us having sex. It has to do with you never mentioning the fact that you were leaving."

The sexual haze clouding his mind lifted and a light bulb switched on. He sighed with relief before he picked up his jeans and pulled them on. He intended to take her into his arms and explain that he had no intentions of ever leaving her. But before he could, she held up a hand.

"Don't touch me."

He stepped back. "Okay, I get why you're mad. And you're right. I should have told you I was heading back to Montana. But I just decided to go yesterday. I was planning on telling both you and Henry before I left tomorrow."

"And you think telling him is going to make you leaving less painful?"

"I know he'll be upset, but it's not a big deal. I'll only be—"

She didn't let him finish. "Not a big deal? Henry loves you. Did you know that? So you leaving *is* a big deal. And don't act like you didn't know what you were doing when you charmed my son with your cowboy stories and 'hey, partner's. Or when you didn't mention a word about leaving before I fell into your bed." She paused and her eyes narrowed. "Or was that your plan in the first place? Charm my son to get me in bed?"

The fact that she thought he would use a little boy to get sex annoyed the hell out of him. "You know that's not true, Paisley. My relationship with Henry has nothing to do with what happened tonight. And you need to calm down before you say something else you don't mean."

Her eyes flared. "Don't you dare tell me to calm down. I won't ever walk on eggshells for another man. If I think something, I'm going to say it."

"And you really think I would use Henry to get to you?"

She studied him for a second before she shook her head. "No. But you did something just as bad. You made a little five-year-old boy fall in love with you when you had every intention of leaving. And that is wrong. Just wrong. And it's as much my fault as it is yours. I knew you were a no-account drifter, but I still stupidly believed you were a man I could trust. A man I could count on. But, once again, I made a huge mistake."

She whirled to leave, but Hayden grabbed her arm and whirled her right back around. "Just for your information, I wasn't leaving for good. I was going back to Montana to settle a few things before I returned."

"Ha! Is that the lie you planned on telling Henry?"

"It's not a damn lie!"

"Really? And why would you come back when you've made no bones about Montana being your home? A home where you no doubt have numerous women you've made empty promises to."

His temper snapped. "There's only one woman I love and made a promise to. And right now I'm damn well regretting it!"

She lifted her chin. "No need to regret it. I certainly won't hold you to it. I don't want a low-down saddle tramp who thinks nothing about breaking my son's—" Her eyes widened. "What did you say?"

He suddenly realized what he'd done. His anger had made him release the truth. And at the worst possible time. He had wanted to tell her he loved her with softly spoken words that came straight from his heart. Instead, he'd blurted it out in anger.

But it didn't make a difference now.

He sighed. "I love you, Paisley. I've loved you from the moment I set eyes on you. But I'm sure you don't believe that either. I thought what happened tonight proved you were starting to care for me—to trust me. But I was wrong. You don't trust me at all, do you? You can't trust me. And I get it. You've been put through too much hell to trust another man. Especially a saddle tramp like me." He swallowed down the pain that had risen in his throat. "I'm sorry I didn't figure that out sooner. Damn sorry."

He waited for her to say something . . . something that would ease the tight pain in his chest. She didn't. She just stared back at him with eyes that held disbelief . . . and sadness. The kind of sadness that gave no hope.

He retrieved her boots and handed them to her. "I'll walk you back to your room."

They didn't talk on the way. She stumbled going up the stairs and he took her elbow to steady her, but he released her quickly. After that, they didn't touch again. When they reached the guest room, she turned to him and spoke in a soft voice he could barely hear.

"So then you *are* leaving."

He didn't want to, but the ache in his heart made him realize he couldn't live in Texas without Paisley. And she had too many demons to give them a chance. At one time, he thought he could help her conquer those demons. Now he realized he wasn't that man. He hoped one day she would find that man. For her sake. And Henry's.

"I'll talk to Henry before I go," he said. "You were right. I shouldn't have let him get so close." He had let his own dreams for the future screw up his logical thinking and now Henry would pay the price. Just the thought of breaking the little boy's heart was like a hard punch to his chest. But maybe there was something he could give Henry before he left. "Before I leave, I'd like to ask you one favor. I'd like to teach Henry how to ride a horse."

Tears welled in her meadow-green eyes and dripped down her cheeks. He had never wanted to make a woman cry, but right now he wished Paisley's tears were for him. He knew they weren't. They were for Henry. He still couldn't stand there and not try to soothe her. But before he could pull her into his arms, she opened the door and slipped inside her room.

He stared at the closed door for a long moment before he turned and headed down the hallway. In his room, he didn't go back to bed. He didn't think he could ever sleep there again. It held too many memories. Grabbing his packed duffel bag and boots, he headed to the bunkhouse. He took the shortcut through the garden. He was so intent on his pain that he didn't notice Stetson until he spoke.

"Couldn't sleep?"

He stopped in his tracks and turned to see Stetson lying in a hammock in his underwear. Teddy was sleeping on his chest and Stetson was using his bare foot to gently swing the hammock back and forth.

"It's the only thing that gets him back to sleep when he's having a restless night," Stetson explained.

Since Hayden was in no humor to talk to anyone at the moment, he quickly made his excuses. "Well, I'll let you get back to it." He started to leave, but Stetson stopped him.

"Before you go, you mind telling me why you're sneaking through my garden half naked with your boots and duffel in hand? I thought you were leaving for Montana in the morning."

"I decided not to leave for a couple weeks." He paused. "Then I'll be leaving for good."

Stetson struggled to sit up in the wobbly hammock while keeping a secure hold on Teddy. "What happened to you coming back here and winning Paisley's heart?"

"There's no way for me to win Paisley's heart. She'll never trust a good-for-nothing saddle tramp."

Stetson studied him. "She said that?"

Hayden thought back on all the hurtful things Paisley had said that night and nodded. "Pretty much."

Stetson pointed to the bench across from the hammock. "Why don't you sit down and tell me what happened from dinnertime—when you both looked like you would combust from sexual tension—to now."

For someone who didn't feel like talking, the words spilled out easily. Leaving out the sex part, he told Stetson everything that Paisley had said. When he finished, Stetson had the audacity to laugh.

"It's not funny," Hayden snapped. "She broke my damn heart."

"I'm sure she did. Lily has said some things to me when we're fighting that hurt like hell. And I get why Paisley was mad. She thought you were running off and leaving her."

"I would never do that. I made her a promise."

"Jonathan made her a lot of promises too and look how that turned out."

"I'm not Jonathan!"

Teddy fidgeted and Stetson sent Hayden a warning look as he jostled his son back to sleep. When Teddy was settled, he spoke. "I know you're not Jonathan. And I think, deep down, Paisley knows that too. Otherwise, she wouldn't have trusted you with Henry. You just blindsided her when she found out you were leaving. So how did she find out?"

"She saw my packed duffel."

"She was in your room?" Stetson's eyebrows lifted. "Did you leave something out, Hay?"

"Nothing that's any of your business."

Stetson grinned. "Ahh . . . well, that explains it. Women are always emotional after they make love."

"It wasn't making love to her." But as soon as the words were out of his mouth, Hayden knew they were a lie. Paisley *had* made love to him. With every hungry kiss of her lips and every sweet caress of her fingers, she'd made him feel loved, cherished . . . and trusted. She hadn't been able to say it with words, but she *had* said it with her body. He'd let her hurtful words drown out all memories of the moments they'd spent in each other's arms. Instead of alleviating her fears and telling her that he'd never leave her, he'd proven her right.

He was leaving her.

"Shit." He ran a hand over his face. "Love is hard."

Stetson laughed. "I could have told you that. But it's also worth it."

Paisley and Henry were worth it. Hayden wanted to jump up and head right back inside and tell her that he *was* the man for her and he wasn't going anywhere until she realized it. But he couldn't go charging upstairs pounding on her door when she was probably already asleep.

"Stet?" Lily's voice pulled Hayden's attention to the patio where she stood. "Is everything okay?" she asked.

"Everything is fine, honey." Stetson tried to get out of the hammock. It looked like it wasn't easy while holding a baby so Hayden got up and pulled him to his feet. Stetson studied him. "You gonna be okay?"

"That depends on whether or not I can convince Paisley I love her."

"So you're staying?"

Hayden nodded. "Thanks for talking me through it."

"No problem." Stetson slugged him in the arm before he turned and headed toward the patio. "That's what brothers are for."

CHAPTER SEVENTEEN

PAISLEY DIDN'T SLEEP well. Her emotions were all over the place. Her body hummed with the aftereffects of the amazing orgasms Hayden had given her while her mind kept replaying their fight. Not that it had been a fight. She had been the only one fighting. She cringed as she remembered how she had thrown her boots at him and all the hurtful things she'd said. He had just stood there and taken it . . . and then told her that he loved her.

Her heart believed him. It was her head that couldn't. How could he love a screwed up woman with trust issues? It made no sense. Nor did her reaction to his words. There had been a moment when she had wanted to fling herself into his arms and absorb his love. A moment when she had wanted to throw caution to the wind and once again believe in happily-ever-afters.

Unfortunately, she couldn't. Hayden deserved better than that. He deserved a woman who could trust him.

So instead of falling into his arms and making empty vows she couldn't keep, she had said nothing. The pain on his face had killed her . . . was still killing her. But it was better to break things off now. If Hayden did love her, he would get over her.

The next morning, she packed her and Henry's bags. She had told Hayden he could teach Henry how to ride a horse, but she realized it would just make Hayden's leaving harder on Henry. He was already too close. When she told him that they were leaving the ranch, he threw a major fit.

"No-o-o! This is my home! This is my home!"

She didn't get after him. She couldn't blame him for wanting a home. Or loving the ranch so much he didn't want to leave. She waited for him to run out of steam before she pulled him into her arms and tried to explain.

"I know you love the ranch, Henry. But this isn't our home. We were just guests here. Now it's time for us to leave and make our own home."

"But I don't want another home. I want this home. Stetson is the boss and he said I could libe here for as long as I want. And I want to libe here forelder."

"Stetson was just being a good host. The King-mans are a family. And we're a family too, Henry. We might not have as many people in our fam-ily as the Kingmans, but I think we have just as much love." She hugged him tightly. "I love you. I love you so much."

His arms came around her. "I lobe you too, Mama, but I don't want to leabe. Hay will miss me. He will miss you too."

Paisley blinked back the tears. "I know he will,

but Hayden has a family too. He has a mama and a daddy in Montana. I'm sure he's ready to get back there and see them."

Henry pulled back and stared at her. "Hay is leabing?"

She smoothed his hair and nodded. "Yes, honey."

Henry's eyes held pain and confusion. "But he was gonna be my stepdaddy."

It was a struggle to talk around the lump in her throat. "I know, but it's going to be okay. We're going to be okay." She didn't know who she was trying to convince. Henry or herself.

The Kingmans seemed as upset about them leaving as Henry was. They all tried to talk her out of it. Except for Stetson. He didn't say anything until she and Henry said goodbye, then he took her hands and gave them a gentle squeeze.

"I want you to know that you and Henry will always have a home here."

Paisley could only nod as she struggled to hold back her tears. She felt like crying even more as the castle grew smaller and smaller in her rearview mirror. By the time they got to Hester's, all it took was Hester meeting them at the door for the dam to break and Paisley to burst into tears.

"See!" Henry yelled. "You didn't want to leabe the ranch either, Mama. And now we're both sad."

Hester pulled Paisley into her arms and patted her back as she spoke to Henry. "Go on into the kitchen, Henry. I made you some snickerdoodle cookies. They're on the table. And Wish has been waiting all morning for you to get here."

The promise of cookies and a cat had Henry

heading to the kitchen. When he was gone, Hester drew Paisley over to the couch and sat her down before handing her a tissue from the box on the coffee table.

Paisley wiped at her cheeks. "I'm so sorry, Hessy. I didn't mean to fall apart as soon as I stepped in the door."

"No need to apologize. Sometimes a good cry untangles all the confusing emotions and makes you see things clearly." She hesitated. "I'm assuming those emotions have to do with Hayden."

Just his name had tears welling. Paisley's voice quavered as she spoke. "H-H-He says he's in love with me."

"And you don't believe him?"

"I don't know what to believe. And even if he does love me, it doesn't matter because I don't know if I can ever trust a man again. And you have to have trust for a relationship to work."

"Bull hockey."

Paisley blinked. "Excuse me?"

Hester handed her another tissue. "I don't know anyone who trusts their partners completely. Take your sister for example. Chance is a preacher. You'd think if any man was trustworthy, it would be him. But when Darcy Hill said she needed Chance to counsel her after her husband dumped her, your sister said 'Oh, hell no!' and with good reason. Everly knows Chance adores her, but she still wasn't willing to tempt fate. Everyone in town knows why Darcy's husband dumped her. Now, I'm not saying that trust isn't important to a relationship. I'm just saying it's not the most important thing. The most important thing is forgiveness. If you're going to make a relationship work, you have to learn how to forgive. That's your biggest problem, Paisley. You can't forgive."

"But Hayden didn't make any mistakes I need to forgive him for. He's been the sweetest man ever. He's been patient and loving with both me and Henry."

Hester studied her with her penetrating violet eyes. "I wasn't talking about forgiving Hayden. I was talking about forgiving yourself."

"Myself?"

Hester sighed. "As women, we pride ourselves on being the intuitive gender, the ones who have excellent emotional quotient. When Jonathan turned out to be an abuser, it made you completely lose faith in your ability to choose a good partner. It's not men you don't trust. It's yourself. Until you can forgive yourself for choosing Jonathan and realize that love is always a gamble—it's never a sure bet—you won't be able to accept love from anyone. Or give it."

Paisley felt like Hester had hit her right between the eyes . . . with the truth.

After confronting Jonathan, she had gotten her power back, but she still hadn't forgiven herself for choosing him in the first place. She had thought she would never trust men again, but it was her own decision-making she might not ever be able to trust again. It was a terrifying thought.

"And how do I do that? How do I learn to trust my decisions?"

"By understanding you're human. You aren't

always going to make the best decisions. In fact, you're going to make a lot of mistakes. We all do."

"But making a bad choice on a man to share my life with doesn't just affect me. It affects Henry. And I already screwed up once. I can't do that to Henry again. I won't." She had never asked Hester to read her palm—probably because she was too scared at what Hester would see—but she asked her now. She held out her hand. "Can you see my future, Hessy? Can you tell me what it holds and what I need to do?"

Hester took her hand, but she didn't look at it. "You don't need me to tell you what to do, Paisley. Deep down, you know what's right for you and Henry. You just need the courage to go for it." She squeezed her hand. "Now why don't you head on upstairs and take a nap. You look exhausted."

With her thoughts running rampant, Paisley didn't think there was any way she'd be able to sleep. But as soon as she lay down on the bed in the guest room, she fell into an exhausted slumber. She didn't wake until it was dinner-time. Henry was still mad at her for taking him away from the ranch. As soon as she walked into the kitchen, he stopped chattering at Hester and glared at her. He continued to glare at her while they ate. Once he was finished eating, he asked to be excused and raced upstairs to his room.

"He'll get over it," Hester said as they cleaned up the dishes. But Paisley had to wonder if he would. She certainly didn't feel like she would get over leaving the ranch. She already missed it terribly. Or maybe what she missed was Hayden.

When the dishes were finished, Hester took off her apron and hung it up. "I'm going over to Kitty's for a couple hours. We're working on quilts for Delaney and Shane's babies." She snorted. "Although I do most of the quilting while Kitty does most of the talking."

After Hester left, Paisley checked on Henry playing in his room before she sat downstairs in the dark and tried to unscramble her feelings. Hester was right. She didn't trust herself to choose a good man. She had screwed up before. It only made sense that she would screw up again.

She thought back to Jonathan's proposal. They had been at a New Year's Eve party at the country club when he'd gotten down on one knee and pulled out a ring. Her first gut reaction hadn't been thrilled excitement. It had been stunned shock, followed quickly by panic. She had glanced around at her parents and Jonathan's parents and their neighbors and friends. They all had beaming smiles and looks of expectation. Paisley had always prided herself on meeting people's expectations.

So she'd said yes. She'd said yes, even when her heart had been telling her no. Then Henry had arrived and all she'd wanted was for him to have a family with two loving parents. Once again, she ignored what her gut had been telling her. It didn't matter if she got hit occasionally as long as Henry was happy. If Jonathan hadn't threatened Henry, Paisley would probably still be with him . . . a man she had never loved. Or chosen. A man who had never made her feel anything but fear.

Memories of the night before came flooding back. Hayden had made her feel a lot of things. Beautiful and desirable. Empowered and in control. Worshipped and worthy. But the main thing he had made her feel was safe. So safe she felt comfortable releasing all her emotions. She had never yelled at anyone like she had yelled at Hayden. And he had taken it. He had taken all her hurtful words and still told her that he loved her.

That was love.

"Oh, Hayden," she whispered. "I've been such a fool."

She would continue to be a fool if she didn't try to fix the mess she'd made of things.

Jumping to her feet, she grabbed her purse and started for the door before she remembered Henry was upstairs playing. She wasn't about to take him to the ranch with her and get his hopes up. Especially when Hayden might not be receptive to her apology. He might even be gone.

As soon as the thought entered her head, she pushed it back out.

Hayden wouldn't leave town. He had made a promise to teach Henry how to ride a horse and he would keep that promise. That was just the type of man he was. He was a man you could trust . . . a man she could trust.

She headed up the stairs to get Henry ready for bed. Once he was asleep and Hester was back, she'd head out to the ranch. She was scared, but in a good way. The kind of scared you got when you had made a decision and all that was left to do was to take the plunge.

When she got to Henry's room, he wasn't there. Figuring he was in the bathroom, she headed down the hallway. But he wasn't there either. Nor was he in her room or Hester's. Hurrying back to his room, she checked under the bed and in the closet before her gaze caught on the window.

It was wide open.

"Henry!" she yelled as she hurried to the window. It was too dark to see anyone in the yard below. "Henry! Henry!"

When he didn't answer, she headed back downstairs. By the time she got outside, her heart was beating frantically. She searched all around the house and in any places a child might hide. But she knew he wasn't hiding. He'd done what he'd done before. He'd gone to see Hayden. But this time, Hayden wasn't across the street at the bar.

This time, he was miles away at the Kingman Ranch.

CHAPTER EIGHTEEN

THERE WAS A reason Hayden hadn't wanted to tell the Kingmans who he was. The proof of his fears was staring back at him right now. There was anger or suspicion in every eye trained on him. Except for Stetson's and Uncle Jack's. They weren't looking at him at all. Nor had they said a word since Hayden had called everyone into the family room after dinner to tell them who he was. They both just sat in chairs in front of the fire, sipping whiskey. Uncle Jack in a tall-back chair that had once been King's and Stetson in the overstuffed chair.

"Okay," Delaney said. "Let me get this straight." She was sprawled out on the couch with her feet up and her large stomach protruding like an overfilled beach ball. "Your mama worked as a maid in this house and our daddy got her pregnant. When he didn't want to acknowledge his child—surprise, surprise—she ran off to Montana and had you."

Buck, who was sitting on the couch next to Delaney, pointed a finger at Hayden. "That's why you remind me of Stetson. You have Kingman blood running through your veins."

"So he claims." Wolfe stood at the fireplace with his eyes narrowed on Hayden. Of all the Kingmans, he was the angriest. "What proof does he have other than his word? And I don't trust a man who has been lying to us all along."

"Like Buck said, any fool can see he's a Kingman," Uncle Jack grumbled. "I knew it from the moment I set eyes on him. If you have bad eyesight, boy, that's your problem."

"So that excuses him from not telling us—acting like he was just some ex-rodeo cowboy who needed a job."

"I am an ex-rodeo cowboy," Hayden said.

"But you didn't need a job. You have land in Montana."

"Just 'cause you have land doesn't mean you don't need a job," Uncle Jack said. "And he sure has worked his tail off for this family. If he hadn't shown up, you wouldn't have had all the time off to hang out with your daughter. Not only did he take over for you on the ranch, but also at the bar. And he's freed up more time for everyone else as well."

"But why didn't you tell us who you were to begin with, Hayden?" Delaney shifted on the couch. As she struggled to get comfortable, she almost kicked Buck.

"Hey! Watch it, Del." Buck grabbed her foot. But instead of shoving it away, he rested it on his lap and massaged it as his gaze returned to

Hayden. "Maybe you wanted to scope us out first and see how much money you could get."

"I don't want your money," Hayden said.

"Then what do you want?"

"Nothing."

"Then why did you come?" Delaney asked.

Adeline rose from her chair and spoke for the first time. "He came because he wanted to know who his family was. Right now, we're acting like a bunch of arrogant, untrusting fools."

"Because we treated him like family and he lied, Addie!" Wolfe snapped.

"As if you have never lied, Wolfe Kingman." Adeline glanced around the room. "I think we've all told lies for one reason or another." She looked back at Hayden. "But you should've told us sooner, Hayden."

He nodded. "You're right. I should have. But I didn't want to disrupt your lives. Douglas was your daddy. I can live with what he did to me because I had a stepdaddy who showed me what a father could be. But y'all . . ." He let the sentence drift off. Stetson finished it for him.

"But we didn't."

Hayden sighed. "I didn't want to make Douglas's memory any worse than it already was."

"Why are you telling us now?" Buck asked.

Stetson fielded the question. "Because I figured it out. I overheard Hayden talking to Henry in the stable about him not having a good father and his mother remarrying his stepfather. I had already noticed the similarities between Hayden and me and put two and two together."

"So now I have four annoying brothers to deal with?" Delaney had sat up and was rubbing her stomach.

Hayden shook his head. "I'm not planning on pushing my way into your family. I didn't even plan on staying for as long as I have."

Wolfe studied him. "Then why did you stay so long?"

It was a good question. Hayden could say it had to do with Paisley and Henry. But as he looked around the room at the Kingmans, he realized there was more to it than that. "I never had siblings so I guess it was kind of nice to be around y'all."

Adeline walked over and gave him a tight hug. "We've become attached to you too, Hayden." She drew back and looked at her siblings. "Don't even try to act like y'all haven't. All I've heard since Hayden showed up is what a godsend he's been and how much y'all like him. And how you hope he'll stick around because you've never seen a man better with horses. Well, now we know why. Horses are in his blood. Just like they're in ours." She hooked her arm through his. "Hayden is our brother. And instead of sitting here and acting like a bunch of pouty babies because he sprung a surprise on us, we need to be welcoming him to the family."

"Speaking of babies—" Delaney started, but Stetson cut her off.

"Addie's right." He got up from his chair and held out a hand to Hayden. "Welcome to the family, Hay."

Hayden didn't know why tears welled in his eyes, but there they were. He blinked them away as he took Stetson's hand. Buck got up and shook his hand next. After a warning look from Stetson, Wolfe begrudgingly came over. His handshake was much tighter than Stetson's. In fact, it was downright painful.

"You better not be lying now."

"I give you my word that I'm not. I don't want anything from your family, Wolfe. In fact, as soon as I find a piece of land here in Texas, I plan to quit and start my own ranch." Hopefully, with the woman of his dreams.

But that wasn't looking promising. Paisley and Henry were gone. When he'd found out they'd left the ranch, he'd almost started weeping like a baby. He'd been terrified that they had left Cursed and he only started breathing again when he found out they were staying at Hester's. Once he got things settled with his family, he intended to go calling and let Paisley know that he wasn't going anywhere.

"Well, that's chickenshit." Wolfe's words pulled him out of his thoughts. When Hayden shot him a confused look, he continued. "You heard me. It's chickenshit to run off and start your own ranch when we just learned about you. As your little brother, it's my duty to make your life miserable. If you don't believe me, ask Stetson. And I can't do that if you're living on another ranch."

Hayden grinned. "Then I guess you'll have to figure out how to squeeze in all that misery before I leave."

Wolfe hesitated. "Or figure out how to get you to stay."

"Damn straight," Buck said. "You can't go, Hay. You're part of the family now. Which means you're stuck with us." He glanced at Delaney. "Even the annoying ones."

Hayden waited for Delaney to get onto her brother. She didn't. She just sat there holding her stomach with a strange look on her face. Hayden didn't know a lot about pregnant women, but he knew something wasn't right.

"Del?" he said. "Are you alright?"

It took a second for her to answer. "Hell, no, I'm not alright. And if y'all can quit yakking for two seconds, I would have told you that I'm having major contractions. But this family doesn't listen to anyone. Y'all are a bunch of know-it-all, cocky—" She cut off and squeezed her eyes closed.

Everyone in the room shot into action. Adeline rushed to her sister's side. Buck yelled that he'd get the car. Wolfe ran to get Shane. Stetson called the doctor. And Hayden stood there not knowing what to do. His focus was so intent on Delaney he almost didn't notice his phone vibrating in his pocket.

When he saw Paisley's name on the screen, he almost dropped his phone as a mixture of love and hope surged through him. But as soon as he answered, he knew she wasn't making a social call. There was fear and desperation in her voice.

"Hay-den?"

He moved out of the great room and into the foyer. "What happened?"

"It's Henry. He ran away and I think he might be on his way to the ranch."

"Henry ran away and he's on his way to the ranch? How?"

"I don't know. I just know he was really upset about leaving you and now I can't find him anywhere."

Hayden's heart dropped at the thought of Henry walking alone on the edge of the highway. Or worse, taking a ride from some stranger. "How long has he been gone?"

"I'm not sure. He went up to his room just a little over an hour ago. So it couldn't be more than that."

"It's going to be okay," he said with as much conviction as he could muster when his heart beat out of control. "We're going to find him. I'll get in my truck and start looking for him. I'm assuming you called the sheriff and Everly and they're looking for him too."

"No, but I will. You were the first person I thought to call."

The fact she had called him first, even before her sister, might have made him happy if he hadn't been so scared. "Check every place in town. Nasty's, Good Eats, the church. I'll cover the ranch. Call me if you find him and I'll do the same."

"Hayden?"

"Yes."

Her voice quavered. "I'm sorry."

He was sorry too, but now wasn't the time

for apologies. "Let's just concentrate on finding Henry and then we'll talk." After he hung up, he turned and discovered Stetson and Wolfe standing there.

"Henry ran away?" Wolfe asked.

"Yes. Paisley thinks he might be coming here."

Stetson lifted the cellphone he held in his hand. "I'll call the bunkhouse and get the ranch hands searching for him. Wolfe and I will help too."

"No, you need to be with Del."

"The rest of the family can go with Delaney to the hospital," Wolfe said. "You need our help."

Hayden's heart tightened. "Thank you. I owe you."

Wolfe grinned and thumped him hard on the arm. "There's nothing I love more than my big brothers owing me."

Since they figured a preschooler on foot wouldn't get far in just over an hour, they didn't waste time looking at the ranch. They split up and started searching closer to town. Wolfe and Stetson took the side roads and Hayden took the highway. He drove along it at a slow crawl, ignoring the honking and blaring of horns as people passed him. When he reached Cursed, he decided to check in with Paisley.

The lot next to the Malones' house was packed with vehicles, and people with flashlights were walking up and down the main street. It looked like the entire town had shown up to help. Hayden didn't know how he'd find Paisley in the crowd.

It turned out she found him.

As soon as he stepped out of his truck, she came running toward him. The paleness of her face and concerned look in her eyes answered all his questions. And she must have read his face too because she didn't ask him any questions either. He opened his arms and she walked straight into them. They held each other tight, communicating their fear without words.

Then Hester's voice rang out. "I found him!"

Hayden took Paisley's hand and they both ran toward the house. Once inside, Hester led them up the stairs and then down the hallway to a narrow door. She opened it to reveal a staircase that led up to an attic.

She handed Hayden the flashlight she carried. "I told Henry about Mystic's spring horse in the attic and how I was going to get it down for him. But when y'all moved to the ranch, I figured he'd forget all about it. Obviously, not."

Hayden led the way up the stairs. When they reached the top, he shined the light around until he found the spring horse. Next to it was a little blond-haired boy . . . sound asleep.

Both Paisley and Hayden released their breaths at the same time. He didn't realize Paisley was crying until he heard the soft sob. He switched off the flashlight and slipped it into his back pocket before he pulled her into his arms. He didn't realize he was crying too until she drew back and cradled his face in her hand, gently brushing away his tears.

"I feel like we've been here before," she sniffed.

"Knowing Henry, I figure we'll probably do this a few more times before he's fully grown."

We'll? Had he heard correctly? Or was it just hopeful thinking? He held his breath as she continued.

"I know you're still worried about getting with a woman who has trust issues. And I do have trust issues. I doubt they'll go away overnight. But it turns out that it wasn't men I didn't trust as much as myself. I was worried about making another bad choice. Not for me, but for Henry. But then I realized Henry has already chosen the man he wants for his father." She smiled. "He chose him months ago."

Hayden was thrilled she saw him as a father for Henry, but he needed to make something clear. "I don't want you choosing me just because Henry loves me and you think I'll be a good father, Paisley."

"Henry has nothing to do with the way I feel when I'm with you, Hayden. And that's the God's honest truth. When I married Jonathan, he made a vow to love, honor, and cherish me. Not once in our marriage did he ever make me feel those things. But you have. You make me feel loved and cherished. You make me feel safe and strong. You make me feel powerful and worthy. All my life I've been so busy making other people happy that I lost sight of who I am. But since knowing you, I've felt more like me than I ever have in my life. You've never expected me to change for you. You love me as I am—even when I'm a raging lunatic who was so scared you were leaving I said hurtful things I didn't mean. I think that's the greatest gift anyone can give to another person. To love them regardless of the mistakes they make."

Her words struck Hayden right in the heart. He'd thought he came to the Kingman Ranch to learn about his father. He now realized he had come to learn about himself. It was time he stopped hiding the truth of who he was and started accepting it.

Even if it ruined his chances with Paisley.

"I'm not just a saddle tramp."

Paisley smiled. "I know that. You're the best horseman I've ever seen in my life."

He swallowed hard. "No, I mean I didn't just drift into Cursed. I came here to find out about my daddy. Douglas Kingman."

She stared at him. "Your daddy? But I don't understand."

"My mother worked as a maid at the Kingman Ranch and she had an affair with Douglas and got pregnant with me. I'm the Kingmans' half sibling."

Her eyes darkened and he quickly tried to explain. "I know I should've told you sooner. But I didn't tell anyone. I didn't want anyone thinking I'd come here to claim the Kingman name or land. I don't want either. I just wanted to see the castle my mother spoke about and learn a little about my father before I headed back to Montana." His hands tightened on her waist. "But then I met you. And you blew all those plans to smithereens. I don't care about Montana if you and Henry aren't there. All I care about is making you both happy. But lying to you wasn't the way to go about that. And you're right to be angry at me. I had no business being hurt about you not trusting me when I hadn't been completely truthful with you. I swear I'll never lie to you again if you'll just give us a chance. Just give us a chance, Pea."

Paisley studied him for a long, nerve-racking moment before she spoke. "A wise woman once told me that good marriages aren't built on trust. They're built on forgiveness."

He stared at her as his heart smiled. "Are you asking me to marry you, Pea?"

She thought for a moment. "I guess I am. As good as you are in bed, I'm not looking for a weekend lover. I'm looking for a man who is willing to make vows and keep them. A man who will be there through thick and thin . . . and runaway sons."

Happiness didn't come close to describing the feeling that flooded through Hayden. "Sons?"

"Or a daughter."

"How about one of each? If our daughter looks anything like her mama, she'll need two brothers to watch out for her."

Paisley smiled. "So you're saying you'll marry me?"

Before Hayden could answer, Henry piped up behind him.

"Say yes, Hay! Say yes!"

They turned to see Henry standing there with his hair mussed and his eyes sleepy . . . but happy.

Hayden couldn't help lifting him into his arms and hugging him close.

Henry hugged him back. "Please say yes, Hay. Quick before Mama changes her mind. Women do that. Brooklyn Ann doesn't lobe me or Brendan. She lobes Peter Michael."

Hayden couldn't help grinning. His joy runneth over. Henry was safe and in his arms and Paisley loved him. Although it would still be nice to hear the words. Maybe all she needed was a little prompting.

"I love you, Pea."

She hooked her arms around both him and Henry. "I love you too, Hay." She smiled. "Foreber and eber."

CHAPTER NINETEEN

"IF YOU'VE CHANGED your mind, you'll have to climb out that window like your son. Your groom is downstairs waiting anxiously for his bride and I don't think he'll let you go without a fight."

Paisley turned from the window to see Everly standing in the doorway. Her sister looked stunning in the soft green maid-of-honor dress with her fiery hair piled up on her head . . . and her golden eyes glittering with tears. "Oh my God, Paise. You look beautiful."

Paisley looked down at her dress. It wasn't white. Or off-white. Or any subdued color usually worn by brides. It was a bright floral print with all the colors of her attendants' dresses— Everly's green, Delaney's blue, Adeline's pink, Lily's yellow, Gretchen's red, and Mystic's purple. Six months ago, Paisley would have scrolled right past the colorful dress when she'd seen it advertised on Instagram. But six months ago she was still a woman in hiding. A woman too afraid to draw attention to herself with bright colors and short hems. A woman who had no confidence to be who she was.

But she was no longer that woman. She was strong. She was confident. She was beautiful.

She glanced at the full-length mirror in the corner and smiled at the woman in the flowered dress and red cowboy boots. "I do look hot as shit, don't I?"

Everly laughed as she moved into the room. "Damn, I created a monster."

"You didn't create the monster. You just egg her on. A perfect example is the wedding gift you gave me. A riding crop, Ev? Really?"

Everly gave her an innocent look. "I thought you could use it now that Hayden has taught you how to ride."

"You know Hayden doesn't use crops on horses. And neither would I."

Everly shrugged. "Then I guess you'll just have to figure out another use for it." Her smile faded. "Now back to my first concern. Are you having wedding day jitters and considering climbing out that window?"

After suffering through an abusive marriage, it made sense that Paisley would have wedding day jitters. But her stomach wasn't jumpy with nerves like it had been when she married Jonathan. Today, all she felt was peace and a warm sense of contentment.

"I have no desire to escape, Ev," she said. "I was looking out the window to see if I could see the land Hayden's clearing for our house."

Everly flopped down on the bed. "I don't know why you need a house when you have a big ol' castle."

"Hayden and I want our own space. With the arrival of Kate and Nate." Delaney and Shane's daughter and son. "And Luna Hester." Mystic and Buck's daughter. "This castle is getting a little cramped. Finding a place to be alone is nearly impossible."

Everly smiled slyly. "And yet, I'm sure you two have had no problem. Henry told me all about catching you in the labyrinth. So don't tell me that riding crop won't come in handy."

Paisley cringed at the memory of Henry discovering her and Hayden kissing. Thankfully, things hadn't gotten too steamy. "We were only kissing." She turned to the mirror to reset a hairpin that was coming out of her updo. She ended up jabbing herself in the head when her sister continued.

"According to Henry, you were kissing 'real hard' and Hayden was squeezing your booby.'"

Paisley whirled around to stare at Everly. "He saw that?"

"The kid sees everything. He's better at reporting gossip than Kitty Carson. And he pays extra close attention to whatever Hayden is doing." Everly grinned. "I wouldn't be at all surprised if my nephew doesn't try out 'hard kissing' when he starts kindergarten next month."

"Sweet Lord," Paisley groaned. "I hope you explained that kissing is for adults."

"Sorry, that's not my place. That's his mean

mama and stepdaddy's job. I'm just the fun auntie instigator."

"You just wait." Paisley pointed a finger at her. "Your turn is coming." When Everly got a funny look on her face and placed a hand on her stomach, Paisley's eyes widened. "Ev? Are you pregnant?"

Everly shrugged. "It looks that way."

"Have you told Chance?"

"Are you kidding? When I told him my period was a few days late, the man drove all the way to Amarillo to a twenty-four-hour pharmacy to get me a pregnancy text, then he refused to leave the bathroom while I peed on it. He's over the moon." She hesitated and a smile lifted the corners of her mouth. "And so am I."

"Oh, Ev!" Paisley hurried across the room and pulled her into her arms. "I'm so happy for you." She drew back. "And I want you to know I'm going to spoil the hell out of him or her." She grinned. "Payback is hell."

"You really have become a curser, Paise. When Mama and Daddy hear the way their sweet little angel talks, they're going to be shocked."

Their mother and father had accepted Paisley's invitation to the wedding. She wasn't surprised. The Kingmans were a much more prestigious family than the Stanfords. Her parents wouldn't want the Kingmans thinking they wouldn't come to their own daughter's wedding. That wouldn't look right. Her father had even insisted he walk her down the aisle. Paisley had refused. She was her own woman now and she had no intentions of letting anyone give her away. She'd given her-self away once to a man and she'd never do it again.

She would love and cherish Hayden, but she also intended to love and cherish herself. She'd passed the state nursing exam and would start work this fall at the county hospital. It would be hard to work and be a wife and mom, but she knew she could do it. She could do anything.

"Mama!" Henry's yell had her and Everly turn-ing as a little cowboy strutted into the guest room.

Paisley's heart swelled. Henry looked like a little miniature Hayden in the starched western shirt, stiff Wranglers complete with a belt and big buckle, roper boots, and a black Stetson. She couldn't help scooping him up and giving him a tight hug.

Something he didn't like at all.

He wiggled to get out of her arms. "Stop, Mama. I'm too big to be carried like a baby."

She gave him a big kiss on the cheek before she set him down. "Sorry, but you just look so cute."

He straightened his hat and sent her an annoyed look. "Cowboys aren't cute. They're handsome."

"Yeah, Paise," Everly said. "Don't you know anything?" She winked at Henry. "You're lookin' mighty handsome there, cowpoke."

"Thanks. You look nice too—I mean you look pretty. Hay says girls don't like it when you say they look nice." He lifted his chin and quoted his hero. "'If you can't think of a better word to describe a lady, then don't say anything at all.'"

"And Hay would be right." Everly tapped the brim of his hat.

He scowled. "Watch it, Aunt Everly. Cowboys don't like people touching their hats."

Paisley stared at Henry. "What did you say?"

"I said that cowboys don't like people touching their hats."

"No," Everly said. "My name. Say my name."

"Everly James Ransom."

Everly glanced at Paisley with surprise . . . and a touch of sadness. Paisley understood completely. She had wanted her son to be able to pronounce his *v*'s, but now that he could, she realized how much she was going to miss it.

"I guess our little man is growing up," Everly said.

"I am growing." Henry puffed out his chest. "I grew a whole two inches this summer. Didn't I, Mama?"

He had. Paisley wished she could keep him her baby forever. But she knew that wasn't possible. He would grow up. He'd grow up to be a good man. She and Hayden would make sure of it.

"Hay said in a couple summers I should be big enough to help with the roundup," he continued. "Especially since I can already ride a horse all by myself." With Hayden riding right next to him the entire time. Henry beamed as he tucked his thumbs into his belt. "I'm a real cowboy. But right now, I'm on official ring bear bid-ness."

"Ring bearer," Paisley corrected. "And please don't tell me you lost the rings."

"Nope." He patted his front pocket. "I got them right in my pocket. I'm here because Hayden sent me. He said to tell you that he can't wait another second to become your husband." He grinned. "And my stepdaddy." He took her hand. "So come on, Mama. Let's get married."

"You're gonna wear a hole in that expensive rug, son."

Hayden stopped pacing in front of the windows and turned to find Jimmy standing there. Jimmy and Hayden's mama had gotten to the ranch a few days ago. Hayden had been worried the castle would hold bad memories for his mother. And there had been an awkward moment when he'd first ushered her and Jimmy through the big doors and she'd come face-to-face with the entire Kingman clan. But then Uncle Jack had shuffled forward and pulled her into his arms. "Welcome back, Catherine. You raised yourself a fine son." That was all it had taken for the awkwardness to evaporate.

In the days that followed, his mama did what she did best and started mother-henning all the King-mans and spoiling all the babies like they were her own grandkids. While Jimmy had helped out on the ranch and joined in on Potts and Uncle Jack's late night domino games. Hayden's worry that his stepdaddy would feel hurt about him coming to the Kingman Ranch was ungrounded. Jimmy understood why Hayden had wanted to find out about his biological family.

He also understood just how nerve-racking getting married was.

"Here, this might help." Jimmy held out a glass of whiskey.

Hayden took the glass and downed the fiery liquid in one slug. Once the burning had stopped, he asked, "Were you this nervous when you married Mama?"

"Yep. I wasn't just terrified of not being able to give her everything she needed. I was terrified of not being able to give you everything you needed."

As always, Jimmy had hit the nail directly on the head. Hayden was terrified. In the last five months, he'd come to love Paisley and Henry more than he ever thought possible. They were his entire world and the thought of disappointing them was almost too much to bear.

"What if I can't be the husband Paisley needs and the father Henry needs?" Hayden asked as he white-knuckled the glass.

"If the way they love you is any indication, I think you've already proven you can give them what they need."

"But what if I screw up?"

Jimmy sighed. "Believe me, you will. I screwed up a lot after I married your mama."

"No, you didn't. You were the best husband and father a man can be."

Jimmy was a good head shorter than Hayden, but his words of wisdom had always made him seem ten feet tall. "That's the great thing about love, son. When you love someone, you overlook all their faults and just see the good in them. Paisley and Henry love you. Love them back with all your heart and the rest will just fall into place."

It didn't matter that all the Kingman groomsmen and Chance were standing around in the family room waiting to head to the garden for the wedding. Hayden eyes filled with tears as he leaned in and hugged his father. "Thanks, Dad."

"Anytime, son." Jimmy pulled him close and thumped him on the back. "You got this."

"Of course he's got this," Uncle Jack said from King's chair, proving that he'd been eavesdropping on their conversation. "You just need to treat a woman like you would a horse. Ride them hard and never put them to bed wet."

"I get the riding hard part," Buck said. "But I don't get the putting them to bed wet part." Both he and Shane were stretched out on separate leather sofas. The two men were still dealing with fussy babies getting them up at all hours of the night and seemed to be continually tired. In fact, Shane was sound asleep and snoring softly.

"He means don't let your wife go to bed madder than a wet hen," Wolfe said as he reached over and shoved Buck's boots off the couch. "And I can attest to the fact that it's a bad idea. If Gretchen goes to bed mad, I'm likely to catch holy hell the next morning."

"Or be given the silent treatment," Stetson said. "Which is even worse. When Lily isn't talking, she's steaming mad."

"It's not the silent treatment that freaks me out with Adeline," Gage said. "It's when her voice gets real soft." He spoke in a soft voice that sounded very similar to Adeline's. "'Of course I'm not mad, honey. Why would I be mad? In fact, why don't you head on out to the bunkhouse and play some poker with the ranch hands. I'm sure you'll enjoy their company more than you do mine.'" He shook his head. "Which I've come to figure out means—I'm mad as hell and you should know why I'm mad as hell. And if you don't figure it out and start apologizing, I'm going to kick your ass out of our bed and you can go sleep in the bunkhouse with the other clueless men."

Jimmy laughed and shot a glance over at Hayden. "It looks like you have plenty of people to give you advice about keeping your woman happy."

Before Hayden could reply, Henry came charging through the door like the new Wranglers Hayden had bought him were on fire. "Me and Mama are ready to marry you, Hay!" He dove straight at Hayden, trusting that he'd catch him. And Hayden always would.

Just like that, Hayden's nerves disappeared.

"Then let's go get married, partner."

The wedding was held in the garden. In late July, it bloomed in a profusion of color. But it didn't come close to being as beautiful as Hayden's bride. Paisley looked like a stunning bouquet in the short, full-skirted dress. Her hair was pinned up in a cluster of golden curls with delicate flowers interwoven in the sunshine strands. Her spring-green eyes were bright . . . and loving.

When she reached him, he took her hands in his and smiled. "Hey, Sweet Pea."

She returned his smile and said his name in a way that always made him feel weak-kneed. "Hay."

They repeated the vows they had written without a single hitch, but the ring portion of the ceremony was delayed when Henry couldn't get the rings out of the pocket of his stiff jeans. When Chance pronounced them husband and wife and they went to kiss, their lips barely touched before Henry wiggled his way between them and yelled,

"Can you wait to kiss Mama hard, Hay? 'Cause being a ring bear has worked up my appetite."

Everyone laughed and Hayden figured he could wait a little longer to kiss his wife hard. It wasn't until much later that he finally got Paisley alone. Her hair had fallen down from its fancy updo while they had been dancing and the sunshine waves fell around her face as he pulled her down the steps that led to the labyrinth.

"Just where are you taking me, Mr. West?"

"To have my wicked way with you, Mrs. West."

Her fingers tightened around his. "Maybe I'll have my wicked way with you."

Hayden picked up his pace. Paisley had become a lot more aggressive during their lovemaking. And he liked it. He liked it a lot.

Unfortunately, his plan to get her alone didn't work out.

When they got to the secret garden, it was filled with Kingmans who looked like they'd had the same idea. All the men carried bottles of champagne and glasses like Hayden did. All of them looked just as disappointed.

Stetson sighed. "Well, since we're all here . . . and with plenty of champagne." He popped the cork on the bottle he held. "We might as well make a toast."

"Not just a toast," Adeline said. "Let's also make a wish. A wish that this family will continue to stick together through thick and thin."

After the champagne was passed around and Stetson made a toast to Paisley and Hayden's long and happy marriage, the men dug through their pockets for change. When everyone had a coin, they encircled the fountain and made that wish.

It came true.

Through good times, and bad times, the King-mans stuck together . . . and lived happily ever after.

THE END

POTTS'S FAMOUS FRENCH TOAST CASSEROLE

10 cups of cubed bread or enough to fill a 9x13 baking dish (I use brioche, but you can use regular white, wheat, or French too)

5 eggs
1 cup whole milk
1 cup heavy cream
½ cup brown sugar
½ cup sugar
2 teaspoons vanilla
2 teaspoons cinnamon
½ teaspoon salt
Powdered sugar and maple syrup (optional)

Place bread evenly in a buttered 9x13 baking dish. Whisk eggs, milk, cream, brown sugar, sugar, vanilla, cinnamon, and salt in a bowl. Pour over bread and push down all the bread pieces until soaked. Then cover with plastic wrap and place in refrigerator overnight. In the morning, place the casserole in a 400 degree oven for 20 or 25 minutes or until golden brown. If middle still isn't cooked through, cover with aluminum foil and cook an extra 5 or 6 minutes. Sprinkle with powder sugar and drizzle with maple syrup if desired. Potts and Katie Lane hope you and your family enjoy!

ACKNOWLEDGMENTS

Where does the time go? It seems like only yesterday that Jimmy and I were driving through Texas and looked up to see a castle-style house sitting on a hill. It got me to thinking . . . what if there was a castle on a ranch? And what if inside that castle there was a family of cowboy princes and cowgirl princesses who needed to find their happily ever afters? The Kingman Ranch series was born! I can't tell you how much fun I had giving the Kingman family their fairytale stories. It's hard to say goodbye to all my beloved characters who have entertained me (and, hopefully, you) for the last couple years. Thankfully, all we have to do to return to the Kingman Ranch and Cursed, Texas, is open a book.

Which brings me to my thank yous. Thank you to my devoted readers for buying my books. I can't tell you how much your support and love mean to me. (Yes, there will be another hot Texas cowboy series coming your way soon!) Thank you to my reviewers for taking the time to tell other people about my stories. Thank you to my beta readers, Margie Hager, Teresa Fordice, and Christy Poling, for catching all my little (and big) bloopers. Thank you to my copyeditors, Rebecca Cremonese and Imogen Howson, for making this series as perfect as it could be. Thank you to my editor, Lindsey Faber, for keeping my characters and storylines on track. Thank you to Kim Killion for my amazing covers. Thank you to Jennifer Jakes for your help with cover copy, formatting, and so much more. And last, but certainly not least, thank you to Jimmy, my daughters, my son-in-laws, and my grandkids for being the bestest family ever and putting up with me always having my head stuck in LaLa Land. I love you more than words can say.

OTHER TITLES BY KATIE LANE

Be sure to check out all of Katie Lane's novels!
www.katielanebooks.com

Kingman Ranch Series

Charming a Texas Beast
Charming a Knight in Cowboy Boots
Charming a Big Bad Texan
Charming a Fairytale Cowboy
Charming a Texas Prince
Charming a Christmas Texan
Charming a Cowboy King

Bad Boy Ranch Series:

Taming a Texas Bad Boy
Taming a Texas Rebel
Taming a Texas Charmer
Taming a Texas Heartbreaker
Taming a Texas Devil
Taming a Texas Rascal
Taming a Texas Tease
Taming a Texas Christmas Cowboy

Brides of Bliss Texas Series:

Spring Texas Bride
Summer Texas Bride
Autumn Texas Bride
Christmas Texas Bride

Tender Heart Texas Series:
Falling for Tender Heart
Falling Head Over Boots
Falling for a Texas Hellion
Falling for a Cowboy's Smile
Falling for a Christmas Cowboy

Deep in the Heart of Texas Series:
Going Cowboy Crazy
Make Mine a Bad Boy
Catch Me a Cowboy
Trouble in Texas
Flirting with Texas
A Match Made in Texas
The Last Cowboy in Texas
My Big Fat Texas Wedding

Overnight Billionaires Series:
A Billionaire Between the Sheets
A Billionaire After Dark
Waking up with a Billionaire

Hunk for the Holidays Series:
Hunk for the Holidays
Ring in the Holidays
Unwrapped

ABOUT THE AUTHOR

KATIE LANE IS a firm believer that love conquers all and laughter is the best medicine. Which is why you'll find plenty of humor and happily-ever-afters in her contemporary and western contemporary romance novels. A USA Today Bestselling Author, she has written numerous series, including *Deep in the Heart of Texas, Hunk for the Holidays, Overnight Billionaires, Tender Heart Texas, The Brides of Bliss Texas, Bad Boy Ranch,* and *Kingman Ranch.* Katie lives in Albuquerque, New Mexico, and when she's not writing, she enjoys reading, eating chocolate (dark, please), and snuggling with her high school sweetheart and cairn terrier, Roo.

For more on her writing life or just to chat, check out Katie here:
Facebook *www.facebook.com/katielaneauthor*
Instagram *www.instagram.com/katielanebooks*

And for information on upcoming releases and great giveaways, be sure to sign up for her mailing list at *www.katielanebooks.com*!

Printed in Great Britain
by Amazon

38267474R00129